Thrown Out
Stories from Exeter

Jennie Coughlin

JENNIE COUGHLIN

Copyright © 2011 Jennifer A. Coughlin

All rights reserved.

ISBN-13: 978-0-9840091-8-3

DEDICATION

In memory of Grampy and Mrs. Rapko,
who inspired me to write.

Dedicated to my mom, for cheering me on at every step;
to Kyrie, for feeding my plot bunnies and corralling them
when they run rampant; and to Jesse Stern,
for showing me the tools to tell better stories.

JENNIE COUGHLIN

THROWN OUT: STORIES FROM EXETER

CONTENTS

Acknowledgments 7

Bones of the Past 11

Thrown Out 20

End Run 53

Intricate Dance 67

JENNIE COUGHLIN

ACKNOWLEDGMENTS

It's been 10 years since Exeter and the characters that call it home first started showing up in my brain, and many people have helped me along the way and deserve thank yous.

My parents have been there since I won my first writing contest in second grade and never questioned my desire to write for a living. They once said to reflect on this when I won my first Pulitzer: "remember all that we have tried to teach you" — and I do for they did it both well and with love. I'm incredibly lucky to have them as parents.
Kyrie has been friend, cheerleader, editor, taskmaster, and sometimes shares part of my brain. She's supported me in a million different ways in the 12 years we've worked together. This book wouldn't exist without her.

I've been lucky to learn from several different writers, in person and through other media, over the years. Don Murray's book is still my go-to reference for writing tips. Professor Roger Gafke told me to never settle for getting by on talent, but instead to always try and get better and learn from those who could teach, and I still try to do that. Steve Binder shared lots of information about the challenges de-aging a character into the past that I relied on while writing Intricate Dance. Mike Lopresti's suggestions for finding and telling good stories work as well for fictional characters as they do for athletes. And Jesse Stern has helped me hone my storytelling skills more ways than I can count. Most of the advanced tools in my storytelling toolbox come from him.

The people behind Rory's Story Cubes and author Mark Bruno started me on the weekly Story Cubes Challenge, which provided the inspiration for some of these stories. Without the Story Cubes and Mark, I would never have thought to do a short story collection for Exeter. Several writing friends have been unfailingly supportive, especially those who read early drafts and made suggestions. Stacey, Sandy, Briana, Libi, Anika, Sherry, Colleen, Barb, and Shannon. You ladies are amazing.

THROWN OUT: STORIES FROM EXETER

JENNIE COUGHLIN

THROWN OUT: STORIES FROM EXETER

BONES OF THE PAST

Riordan shifted his weight in the wicker chair. The fall afternoon was just starting to cool as a breeze blew the first of the season's brilliant leaves across the yard. It felt good after spending the afternoon weeding the flower bed. He still needed to put away his tools, but right now it was nice to sit. It wouldn't be too many more weeks until sunny days and trees tipped with color gave way to dark nights and bare, black branches. He sighed, then thought of all the things he enjoyed about late fall days that led into winter — the warmth giving way to cold, crisp air and the smell of smoke from chimneys and burning brush. Instead of lazy evenings on the porch telling stories to friends and neighbors who stopped by, he'd be settled in at Corcoran's pub, a glass of ale in his hand and a fire in the fireplace. Porch or pub, it didn't matter. They would stop by, ask him to spin a tale or two. Old friends, relatives — both close and so distant it would takes ages to trace the connection — even the occasional college student who didn't mind listening to an old man ramble.

Sometimes there were new faces to add to the familiar, people who hadn't yet heard all the stories Riordan had told time after time. One was walking down the street now. Ellie waved as she approached, her dress slacks and button-down shirt a sure sign she had just come from the Historical

Society's office. The girl worked too hard, slaving away on a Saturday. Anybody else would have at least softened their dress a bit, worn something more comfortable. She was an odd one, so different from dear Becca it was impossible to believe they were related. Not that they were, of course, not by blood.

He called across the yard, "Ellie, dear, come keep an old man company for a few minutes."

She smiled, her wide mouth transforming her face into something full of joy. "Can I get another story if I ask nicely?" Her lips twisted in an impish smirk, and Riordan was reminded of her mother.

"Have you ever known me not to have a story ready to tell?" He motioned her to have a seat in one of the other chairs, and she took it, unclipping her cellphone and setting it on the table between them. She leaned her briefcase against the chair and settled back.

"You're like an unending storybook." She grinned. "I keep thinking you'll run out of stories one of these days, but Aunt Becca says you never have."

Riordan chuckled. "I don't know if I'd go that far — I tell the same tales many a time. But nobody seems to mind."

"Oh!" She sat up. "Maybe you know this. Mrs. Boylan stopped by today to donate some papers she'd found in her father's attic. She started talking, you know how she does, and she said something about Dan and dead bodies in the marsh, but didn't explain." Ellie flushed. "I was busy, and she goes on and on, so I didn't want to ask. And I wasn't quite sure if I should ask Dan about it - I couldn't tell from her comments. It didn't sound like it was anything to do with the mill project, so I wasn't sure it was any of my business. But it keeps skittering around in my head, like a bug I can't quite catch."

"Ahhh... the dead bodies in the marsh." Riordan nodded. "One of the most notorious chapters in Exeter's history. I'm surprised Becca never told you." He paused. "Oh, but she wasn't around. It was the year she was on sabbatical."

THROWN OUT: STORIES FROM EXETER

"So how did bodies get into the marsh?" Ellie asked, then frowned. "And what did Dan have to do with it? He's a few years younger than I am - he must have been in middle school if it was while Aunt Becca was on sabbatical."

"Well, now that's a story you should hear." Riordan thought for a second. "Way back when I was a boy, you never went to play in the marsh. It's been less hazardous since Dan and Evan turned the whole town upside down with their discovery. But before that... I always wanted to explore, but my mother forbid it. The one time I did sneak down there, Officer Reilly, Dan's great-great-uncle, caught me and dragged me home."

"Is it dangerous?"

"The marsh?" Riordan shook his head. "Oh, I don't doubt there are places where you could get sucked into the muck and need help getting out or that someone could drown there if they wandered into the wrong spot. But the same is true of the quarries on the west end, and we roamed all through them as children. No, the danger in the marsh came from other sources. The marsh was dangerous because of the people who used it for their own nefarious purposes." He tapped the side of his nose.

"When you read books or watch movies featuring mobsters, everything's about the Mafia. The Italians have a reputation as gangsters and not without reason. But in this state, the Irish mob has always been at least as powerful. It's a dark, twisted side of our heritage, one that can be traced back to the Old Country and the abuse suffered at the hands of the English. Many escaped to America hoping for a new life, but crumbling towers and green fields gave way to cramped quarters on germ-laden ships. Those that survived found the Yankee establishment just as oppressive as what they'd left behind. The Puritanical Brahmins frowned upon the music and dancing, the storytelling and drinking that's such a part of our culture. Businesses all over bore signs, 'No Irish Need Apply.' Only in the mills could they find work — dirty, dangerous, ill-paid work. Like other ethnic groups, the

Irish came in waves — families and villages finding towns to settle in, neighborhoods to call their own. Exeter was one of them."

He looked across to where Ellie was leaning forward, eager for more. "In Boston, the Irish organized, trying to keep other people out of their neighborhoods, preserving the new homes they had carved out of city blocks. They didn't want other groups to gain power over them as in the Old Country. This became a matter of survival, and soon Boston had an Irish mob to rival the Mafia. While the Italians expanded south to Providence, competing against and working with the families down there, the Irish mob headed west to Worcester. In both cases, the gangs needed a place where they could meet on neutral turf, someplace halfway in between. Someplace they could use for hiding and for... other purposes."

"Wait, the mob was here?" Ellie sat upright. "In Exeter, the world's quietest town?"

He waved a finger at her. "Don't go thinking that just because we're not some big city like Washington that we're some sleepy backwater. People are people, no matter the place."

Ellie snorted. "Can't argue with that — the past month has been more exciting for me than all last year in D.C." She rested her elbows on her knees, settling her chin on her knuckles. "So the mob used the marsh?"

Riordan nodded. "Many of us in town knew, or at least suspected. Stories were told, whispered from person to person. But the only ones who really knew for sure were the local 'affiliate,' and nobody ever dared ask." He paused. "Certain people you didn't mess with." He shuddered. "Not successfully."

He picked his words carefully. "This is one story I don't tell people. Your aunt's probably the only living person who's heard it, at least from me."

"I won't tell." Ellie folded her hands, her face solemn.

"Old man Donaghue, he had a mean streak. His son Steve-"

Ellie interrupted. "The mill owner? He's seemed so nice every time I've talked to him for the project."

"Yes, that Steve." Riordan turned the discussion back to his story. "Steve was only seven or eight when he brought home a puppy one time. Mutt of a dog. Scruffy, scrappy thing. Steve rescued it from a fight it was quickly losing out in the alley behind O'Learys. He paraded it through downtown, stopping by to show my father. I was clerking for him that summer, earning money to pay for law school. Steve was so excited, he was about to bust. Said he'd always wanted a dog. He was on his way to his pa's office to show him. Not 10 minutes later, my father sent me along with some paperwork for Old Man Donaghue to sign." He sighed. "Always wondered if he knew what was going to happen, sent me along on purpose."

"What did happen?" Ellie chewed her lower lip.

"I got there and didn't see Steve or the dog. Got the papers signed." He shook his head, remembering. "On the way back, I decided to cut through the alley to save time. Steve was at the end of the alley, sitting against the wall of the building next door. The dog was lying next to him, dead." He closed his eyes. "There was no blood, but no neck ever looked like that by Nature's design. And there was a dark mark on the wall, just above the dog's body."

Ellie just shook her head. "No."

"Yes." Riordan nodded. "I stopped and asked him what happened. He shook his head, tears running down his cheeks. I knelt down, getting dust all over my slacks. He told me to go away, to run before his pa saw me. Said he should have known better." Riordan swallowed. This was the part he always found toughest to remember, the part he wasn't proud of. "I told him if he needed help, to go to my father or to come to me. And then I left him there." He sighed. "After that, I always believed the whispers."

"So Steve's father..." Ellie's voice trailed off.

Riordan nodded. "I never wanted to look too closely at what he was involved in, but after that, I heard enough to be sure those links to the mob weren't just rumors. I don't know if he was an enforcer or just provided a place for people to hide when the heat was on in the city, but he was involved. My father warned me not to mention it to the chief - every time somebody tried to get him involved, nothing would happen."

"How did Steve get away?"

"About 20 years ago, Donaghue was fading fast. The mob was moving into drugs, but not around here. The college wasn't big enough back then to be a market, and they couldn't risk the attention from the state." He looked out into the distance. "It was about this time of day when I heard. I was sitting out here, writing a letter to your aunt, catching her up on all the news of the town. I wrote to her almost every day while she was gone."

"She still has the letters." Ellie's voice was soft. "I found them one day, while looking for something else."

"That's something, then," Riordan said. "As long as she still has them, I can hope one of these times she'll agree to marry me." He shook off the thought. "I didn't share much of this with her, didn't want to risk putting anything to paper." He remembered the afternoon. "It was a hot day, one of those muggy August afternoons when it seems as though fall will never come. I'd finished up early at the office, but decided the yard work could wait until later, when it had begun to cool. I sat out here, writing Becca, when young Evan went running past, Dan chasing after him, calling for him to stop. The boys couldn't have been more than 12, maybe 13. Evan's family had just moved to town at the beginning of the summer, down the block from the Reillys."

"Danny?" Riordan shoved back from the table and stood up. "Daniel."

Dan looked at Evan, gaining distance from him by the minute, then slowed and jogged back. "Mr. Boyle?" He looked down the block, where Evan had started to slow. "I really have to go. Evan..." He swiped an arm across his dripping face, leaving a dark smudge.

Riordan looked him over, saw the mud smeared across his legs, caking his battered Chucks. "You've been in the marsh."

Dan scuffed his toe, then stopped, crossing his arms. "So? Me and Evan went exploring."

"You're not running in this heat for the fun of it, are you?" Riordan sighed. "What happened?"

Dan hesitated, looking down the block. Evan had stopped and was walking back. Riordan hadn't met the boy before, just seen him around town. He was tall, lanky — the kind of kid who would be all angles until he got older, started filling out some. He'd heard tell he was the same age as Dan, but Evan had half a head on him. Dan was sturdy, the kind of kid who would be a terror on the football team when he got older. Fearless too, always had been. Anything that could make him run had to be bad.

As Evan walked up, Riordan motioned to the porch. "Come on, sit down before you drop, both of you." Dan headed up the walk, but Evan hesitated.

"I don't know... I mean, I've seen you around town. You're the lawyer, the one down by Town Hall. But..." The boy stammered to a stop, his face pale despite a deep tan.

"You can call your parents if you want." Riordan smiled. "I'll talk to them. But you can ask Danny — I've known him since he was born. His father, too."

Evan nodded, eyes wary, but slipped past him, joining Dan on the steps. Riordan leaned against the railing. "What happened down in the marsh?"

"We..." Dan paused. "We were just poking around. Honest. And then we saw this little shack, and we went to explore, but it was locked."

Evan nodded. "It looked really old, like it might fall apart in a storm, but there were three padlocks on the door, and they weren't rusty at all. And the windows weren't broken, neither."

"Did you look inside?" Even as he asked, he knew the answer. What he didn't know was exactly what had spooked them.

Dan shook his head. *"The windows were high — I couldn't see. But Evan looked."*

"There were a bunch of guns." Evan's words spilled out. *"Machine guns and rifles and pistols, and a bunch of knives, and one of them..."* He faltered. *"It looked like it had blood on it."*

"He yelled, and I jumped back and ended up in the marsh." Dan made a face. *"It was sticky and muddy, and there were a billion mosquitos. I tried to get out, but I kept sinking. My feet were all covered in mud, and they weighed a wicked lot. And then I stepped on something hard, and I climbed back up on the bank. Something caught my toe, though, and I pulled hard and-"*

"It was a skull." Evan shuddered. *"Dan landed on the ground, and the skull rolled away, and it had a hole in the back."*

"That's when we took off," Dan said.

Riordan nodded. *"Smart thinking, lads."* He frowned. Calling the chief was out of the question — Old Mike Mullally turned a blind eye to the goings-on in the marsh. Now the staties, they were another matter. He thought they might pay some attention. But he didn't want the boys involved, didn't want them in danger. *"You boys listen to me. Danny, I'm calling your father, letting him know what you found. Don't either of you boys mention this to anybody. Evan, go over to Danny's house, stay there for now."*

The boys nodded. Dan looked up. *"Am I going to get in trouble?"*

Riordan shook his head. *"I don't think so, Danny-Boy. But I don't want to hear of you two ever going into the marsh again."*

They both nodded. Riordan looked at them and frowned. If anyone took one look at the mud smeared all over Dan, word would get out. *"Hose is around the corner in the side yard. Go clean up, get rid of that mud while I call your father."*

He headed inside and dialed the Reillys' number. Eileen answered, but called Kevin to the phone without asking any questions.

"Riordan?"

"Your boy's been down at the marsh, he and his new friend."

"Hell. They get caught?"

THROWN OUT: STORIES FROM EXETER

"No, but they found a skull. Sounds like the owner of it was shot, and you know what that means, m'boy."

Kevin didn't answer, only muttered curses.

"Look, I'll take care of this, call in the staties. I've got a few friends among the troopers, and they'll make sure it doesn't get brushed under the rug. But can you work it out to keep both boys at your place tonight, until things are underway?" At Kevin's question, he replied, "Evan's parents are new in town, don't know the way things work. They hear about this, they're going to call the chief, and then nothing will happen, same way it's been before. By tomorrow, we can have the troopers out here — then Mullally won't have any control over it."

As Riordan wound up the story, Ellie sat there, her face alternating between shock and horror.

"The police chief was in on it?"

Riordan nodded. "Nobody could ever prove it, but we all knew. He looked the other way too many times. You learned — it wasn't safe to rock the boat around here back then."

"So what did they find?"

"Enough guns to arm a street gang. Dozens of knives. And bodies. The final count was 29, but they never did find all the bones for each of those bodies. There were some who said there could be even more out there." He shook his head. "Everybody knew who was responsible, but they never pinned it on anybody. After all these years, they won't. Donaghue is gone, and Steve's clean."

"You're sure?"

He nodded. "He never liked that side of his pa. After I saw what Donaghue did to the puppy, I kept an eye out, and Steve said a few things to me. He'd wanted out before the bodies turned up, but I was never sure if he'd been able to or if he'd just kept it quiet. But if he wasn't out before, he definitely got out then. Cleaned up the business, made sure none of the buildings or apartments were rented to anybody with a mob connection, and managed not to end up dead."

"So the mob's gone from Exeter now." She smiled.

"As far as we know." More than that, Riordan wouldn't say. Ellie didn't need to know his suspicions. Not yet, anyway.

INTRICATE DANCE

August 2001

Chris walked up the Reillys' driveway, wondering where Dan's truck was. He thought he was on time. He checked his watch, just in case. It wouldn't be the first time he had gotten so lost in the piece he was arranging for one of the jazz ensembles on campus that he'd lost track of time.

Dan's mother stepped outside the back door of the main house, waving to Chris. "Kevin and Dan are running behind," she said. "One of the town inspectors showed up an hour later than he said he would, so they're just finishing up on the job site now. Dan mentioned you two had a date, said to go on up."

"Thanks, Mrs. Reilly."

"How many times do I have to tell you? It's Eileen." She shook her head, but she was smiling. "You are coming to dinner next Sunday, right? It's the last one before Bridget and Maggie leave for college."

"I'll be there." A few more pleasantries, and he was able to escape to Dan's apartment above the contracting business. He understood why Dan liked living there — it was right above work, he'd rather pay rent to his parents than a landlord, and it was easily three times larger than the cramped apartment Chris rented a few blocks from campus.

When Dan walked in a few minutes later, he was dirty and covered in sawdust. "Give me 20 minutes to get cleaned up," he said.

Chris laughed. "Take your time — the movie isn't going anywhere, and I can wait for pizza." He held up the VHS tape he'd brought. Dan nodded and stripped off his T-shirt as he headed for the bathroom.

The shower had stopped when Chris heard somebody knocking on the apartment door.

"Can you get that?" Dan appeared with a towel around his waist, rubbing his curly black hair with another. "It's probably Evan." He disappeared back into the bedroom without waiting for an answer.

Chris opened the door, smiling at the familiar face. Those had been few and far between since spring semester had ended and most of his friends from the college had headed home or to Boston for the summer.

"Hey, Chris. I've got some of the softball equipment for tomorrow's game. Dan said he'd take it." Evan held up a bucket of balls in one hand and turned slightly to show the bag of bats hanging from his other shoulder. "I'm covering a shift so Chief McMahon can be at his granddaughter's birthday party."

"Dan just got home, but he should be out in a minute." Chris reached for the bucket, but Evan waved him off. Chris stepped back, and Evan set the equipment down inside the door.

"Hope everybody who promised shows tomorrow. We're close to having to forfeit." Evan frowned, then looked at Chris. "Hey, you wouldn't be interested in playing, would you? We can still add to the roster."

Chris shook his head. "You don't want me," he said. "I was the kid on my Little League team who hunted dandelions in right field instead of paying attention to the game." He pushed aside memories of his father's disappointment after those games.

Evan laughed. "Tell Dan he's got to hit a few extra home runs since I won't be there to do it for him." Evan straightened up, as tall as Chris. "Hey, Liz is dying to get together with adults who aren't related to us — and she's starting to bug me about meeting you." He grinned and raised his voice. "She says the baby has to spend more time with his godfather."

"Oh, bite me." Dan walked into the room, worn cutoffs slung low on his hips. "She just wants to talk to somebody who can talk back - besides you."

Chris grinned. "Or Colleen's been singing your praises as a baby whisperer." He turned to Evan. "Never fails. When one of the twins starts crying, she hands him to Uncle Dan, and he's happy again."

Dan rolled his eyes. "I'm not the only one. Who usually has the other twin? But she'll stop that when she sees the little tool boxes I'm getting them for Christmas."

"Oh, tell Liz that." Evan smirked. "She'll be all over you for assuming that because they're boys, they'll like tools."

"Hey, Michelle can have one, too." Dan shrugged. "Bridget was always stealing the one Dad made me when we were little."

"Does that mean it's going to be Reilly and Kids instead of Reilly and Son someday?" Chris couldn't help but ask. Mr. Reilly didn't seem like the kind of father to pressure his kids to follow in his footsteps — better than he could say about his own father — but he'd only known the man for a few months.

Dan shook his head. "No, she just liked banging with the hammer. Mikey, maybe. Dad can just add another S to the sign." He shrugged. "You want me to drop the stuff off at your place after the game tomorrow or just hang onto it until Thursday's game?"

"You can send them home with Liz," Evan said. "She was going to bring Michelle down to watch."

"Michelle's three months old." Dan snorted. "She must be really desperate to spend time with adults."

"Hey, there's an idea," Evan said. "Chris, why don't you go to the game? Then Liz will get off my case about meeting you, and you three can go over to Corcoran's after."

Chris hesitated. "I'm..." He tried to figure out a way to refuse without having to explain.

"Yeah, come down to the game," Dan said. "You haven't been to one yet."

Chris shook his head. "That's not a good-"

But before he could figure out an excuse to avoid the game, the town fire siren went off. Two hoots, then four.

Evan frowned. "That's Millville. This time of day, probably a kitchen-" He stopped as the siren sounded again, immediately followed by his beeper. "All-call — gotta go."

Dan shut the door as Evan raced for his truck.

"Millville?" Chris frowned. "I thought I'd finally learned all the towns around here."

"It's not a town, just the name used for the neighborhood across from the old mill complex that separates the college from downtown." Dan headed for the couch, taking Chris' hand and tugging him along.

"Is that where Professor Stone lives?" He thought back. "She had all the grad students over before Christmas, even those of us who aren't in the art department." He sat next to Dan on the couch, sinking back into the cushions, Dan's arm around his shoulders.

"It sounds so weird to hear you call Becca that." Dan grinned. "That's her neighborhood." He frowned. "I hope Evan was right, and it's just a kitchen fire. At this time of day, either nobody's home or they are awake — at least no people are likely to be in danger — but those houses are jewels. It would be a shame to lose one."

Chris shook his head. "OK, Mr. History Major." He traced the white patches below Dan's eyes. "You got burned again — you've got a sunglasses line." His tanned skin was dark against Dan's.

"Ran out of sunscreen." Dan grimaced and held out the arm not wrapped around Chris. The shoulder was ghostly;

the rest of the arm, slightly pink. "This burn isn't too bad, but good thing there's no game tonight. I don't need any more sun." He grinned. "Think I can get a hand rubbing on the aloe?"

"Oh, I think I can help with that." Chris traced the edges of Dan's burn — arms, neck, legs — keeping his fingers light.

"Mmmm." But before Dan could say anything else, his stomach rumbled. "Hold that thought. Let me call for pizza."

He got up and went into the small kitchen, where he called in an order. Chris followed and opened the refrigerator.

"Hey, toss me a can of tonic."

Chris shook his head at the odd term, but passed a can of Coke back. "Nobody told me I'd have to learn to speak Boston when I applied up here."

Dan grinned. "Come to the game tomorrow — after we get something to eat at Corcoran's, we can go out and get ice cream with jimmies."

Chris rolled his eyes. "Normal people call them chocolate sprinkles."

"One thing nobody's ever called me is 'normal'." Dan drained half the can. "Seriously, come to the game. Liz isn't the only one who's been wondering when they're going to meet you."

"I don't... That's not a good idea." He swallowed.

"Why not?" Dan leaned back against the counter. "It's not like this is hard-core sports. It's slow-pitch softball. It's about the only time I can hang out with most of my buddies on the Bulldogs. Between jobs and spending time with their families, they're busy. And if they aren't, I am." He made a face. "I'm glad I only have one more semester. Between classes, studying, and work, I never have enough time for anything else. I hardly have enough time to spend with you." He shook his head. "I can't imagine going back for a master's degree like you."

Chris shrugged. "You don't need one — heck, you don't need this degree for what you do. But to teach at a college, I need to finish the master's and the doctorate. I can't make a living just composing."

"Yeah, like Mom and Dad would have let me skip college. At least I wanted to go, because they would have won that fight." Dan stood up and headed for the living room, grabbing Chris' hand again as he walked past. "Besides, the history comes in handy when I'm trying to restore buildings — I like working on the older houses in town, and I want to do more of it." He flopped down on the couch, tugging Chris after him. "So, you're coming, right?"

Chris leaned into Dan as he searched for the right words. "I..." His fingers traced the scar along his right forearm, the movement so habitual it barely even registered. "I can't."

"You can't?" Dan frowned. "I didn't think you had anything on your schedule until the fall semester prep starts next week. You said this was your one break after all the summer class craziness."

Chris thought about lying, but knew he couldn't do that to Dan. "I'm available. I just..." He made himself just say it. "I shouldn't be there."

"What do you mean, 'shouldn't be there'?" Dan stared at him.

"If I go, people will know we're dating."

"Yeah, so?" Dan frowned. "They know I'm seeing somebody. It's not like it's a big secret."

Chris tried to figure out how to explain it, but finally gave up. "You wouldn't understand."

"You've got that right — I don't understand." Dan pulled back and turned so he was facing Chris, one leg hiked onto the couch. "It's not like anybody expects me to be dating a girl. Ever since I got suspended freshman year of high school for beating up a homophobic idiot, pretty much the whole town knows I prefer guys." He grinned. "Word spreads quickly in Exeter."

"See, that's what worries me." Chris sighed, his fingers still running over the scar. "Everybody knows about you. Not me. And you might be a year or two younger, but you've been out a lot longer than I have. I couldn't even admit to myself I was gay until five or six years ago. I still worry about how people will react when they find out."

Dan ran a hand through his still-damp hair. "What are you talking about? The photographer for the campus paper snapped a picture of me kissing you on Valentine's Day, and it ran on the front page. How much more outed can you get?"

"That's campus. Not town." He sighed. "A lot of things on campus don't make it off campus. And a lot of things that are acceptable on campus aren't when you take them off-campus."

"I can't argue that they're not different." Dan reached over to take his hand, lacing their fingers together. "But nobody's going to give you grief for dating me." Dan looked him in the eye. "Look, I know Virginia wasn't the most open place in the world, but Massachusetts is different. Exeter is different."

Chris sighed. "I'll think about it."

Dan opened his mouth to reply, but the doorbell rang. "Pizza." He got up and came back a minute later with the steaming box. Chris slid the movie into the VCR and turned on the TV, hoping it would be enough of a distraction.

A few hours later, they lay in Dan's bed. Chris looked at the clock and groaned. "I need to leave."

"You can stay, you know."

Chris shrugged. "You've got to get up early for work, and I don't want to run into your parents again. It was awkward enough the last time."

"It was fine the last time." Dan yawned. "When Colleen was living up here before she and Eric got married, it wasn't unusual to see him in the morning."

Chris pulled on his T-shirt. "It's still a little too close to living with your parents to not feel weird. Just because yours are more accepting than mine doesn't mean it's not the standard 'parents knowing we have sex' weird."

Dan yawned again. "I'm 23. They know I have sex. They don't care." He stretched and rolled onto his back. "If the state actually permits civil unions because of that lawsuit this spring, you might have to worry about them asking when we're going to make it legal. But they did the same thing to Eric and Colleen."

Chris wasn't even going to touch the civil unions comment. It was still such a foreign concept, he wasn't about to let himself hope. But he wasn't getting into that at 1 a.m. "Oh, go to sleep," he said.

"See you at the game," Dan said, yawning again.

But Chris didn't go to that game. Or the next one. Or the two after that. He tried, but every time he started toward the field, he found himself turning away. He made excuses to Dan, but it was obvious Dan knew they were just that.

The last time, he had almost made it to the field before turning back. When he mentioned that the next day, Dan had just sighed and asked if he would come to a cookout the next weekend.

"Becca has one every summer — most of her neighborhood and half the town are there," he said. "She specifically told me to bring you, and my family will wonder if you're not there."

Chris thought about it for a second. He'd been to Professor Stone's house before, and she was one of the most approachable professors in the department, if not the entire campus. "I'll go." He rolled his shoulders. "And I really am trying to get to one of your games."

"Uh-huh." Dan didn't say anything else, and Chris winced.

The next night, Chris stood on the corner and listened to the sounds coming from the ballpark down the street. Dan and his friends were there warming up, waiting for the rest of the Bulldogs to finish work and get to the ball field. This was the closest he'd gotten, and he was trying to talk himself into walking that last block. He crossed his arms, the fingers of his left hand tracing the familiar scar on his other arm.

The thick August heat pressed down, too much like two summers ago. He stopped, starting to turn and head back to his apartment, but he couldn't keep doing this. Dan wouldn't be patient forever. Chris took a deep breath and forced himself to keep going, to enter the battered gate in the chain-link fence surrounding the elementary school.

He could see Dan at third base fielding ground balls from his teammates, the edges of his battered Red Sox cap dark with sweat. The pale skin on his arms was a little pink; he must be out of sunscreen again. He spotted Dan's scuffed cooler under the team bench near the first base line. The other team was playing catch in the small strip of grass between the third base line and the fence.

Chris reminded himself that if they didn't know him, they weren't likely to say the things he'd grown up hearing. If they did realize he was Dan's boyfriend, Dan said they would be fine with it. Still, Chris hesitated before making his way over. Not for the first time, he wished he'd been able to explain to Dan why he was so hesitant to come. It was too late now — Dan had just seen him and waved. Chris waved back before heading to the small metal bleachers not far from the Bulldogs' dugout.

Still, he couldn't shake the idea that this was a mistake. There were just a couple of people in the bleachers, mostly in the back row. Chris picked the end of the front row instead. If Dan was right, he wouldn't need to run. Still, he wasn't ready to put himself in a position where he couldn't make a fast exit. Not just yet. He rubbed the back of his neck and reminded himself to relax. This was supposed to be fun. He deliberately stretched out his long legs, the heels of his battered leather sandals scuffing up dust between the patches of grass. The Bulldogs were still on the field, the batter now sending balls into the outfield.

Chris settled in and watched while the team finished batting practice and then moved to the sidelines to toss the ball around while the other team took the field. Dan glugged down half a bottle of water, then tossed it to Evan, who pulled off his ballcap and dumped the remaining water over his head, soaking his blond hair, before dropping the bottle in the trash. Now Chris understood why Dan had filled the cooler with a dozen bottles just for himself before heading out. The August day wasn't unusually hot, but sticky enough to discourage movement, much less vigorous activity like a game. He watched Dan and Evan tossing the ball around, the left fielder bouncing ground balls to Dan, which he returned as pop-ups.

Something broke Dan's concentration, and he looked back toward the diamond. Chris tracked the movement with his eyes. He couldn't hear what the other team's first baseman had said to Dan, but Dan's face hadn't been that red a minute ago.

Chris had never seen Dan get mad before — even the past couple of weeks he'd been more resigned than angry over this whole ballgame stalemate. But a couple of Dan's sisters weren't nearly so restrained, and Chris knew the Reilly temper could be pretty fierce once unleashed. He swallowed — the other guy had a good 50 pounds on Dan, and it wasn't fat. The red-headed man had powerful arms, a barrel chest. And when Dan turned his back on the man, whipping the softball back to Evan, the first baseman took a step toward Dan.

"Ignore him."

Chris turned his head to see a blonde woman making a face, curls springing loose from under her ball cap, as she pushed a baby stroller up to the bleachers. He recognized the face, but couldn't place it, which meant she was a townie, probably somebody who had gone to school with Dan and Evan.

"I'm Liz Czarnecki, Evan's wife." She didn't offer a hand, didn't have one free as she juggled a diaper bag and a purse while setting the brakes on the stroller wheels. "The little one's Michelle. You must be Chris." At Chris' nod, she smiled. "Good. It's about time you showed up. After the last game, Evan had to talk me out of hunting you down to knock some sense into you." She shook her head. "He convinced me to wait — neither one of us wanted you to come tonight, not for your first game. Not against the Pirates."

Chris looked at her. "Why?" He looked out at the field. "It have anything to do with Big Red out there?"

Liz rolled her eyes. "Joe." She unbuckled the baby and lifted her onto her lap. "He's a few years older than us, was a senior back when we were freshmen." Liz kept her voice low. "He and Dan... Let's just say this isn't the first time they've tangled. Won't be the last either." Before she could say more, the teams moved to fill the dugouts. The Bulldogs headed back out, taking the field, as the Pirates came up to bat.

"I suppose one bully is better than a dozen." He had a feeling that Joe might be the idiot Dan had mentioned the night he'd first asked Chris to attend a game. But this wasn't the right time for that conversation, not with so many ears around. He forced himself to focus on the players and the game. Chris scanned the field. "So, softball is basically the same rules as baseball, right? I mean, if I can follow a Sox game, I can follow this."

Liz nodded, bouncing the little girl. "Pretty much." She looked at him. "Not a big sports guy?"

"I was a band geek, not a jock." Chris grinned. "Four years of high school football games because band meant marching band in the fall, and I still don't understand the darn game. I just cheer when Dan cheers. Baseball at least I kind of understand."

"You don't understand football, and you watch with him anyway?" Liz lifted an eyebrow. "Wow. It must be love. No offense, but most of the guys he meets on campus either look down on him because he's in construction or want to go out to party when he's got to study."

Chris felt the tips of his ears burn. "He comes out to jazz clubs with me, even when he'd rather be home watching a game. The least I can do is watch football with him, even if I don't get the point of pre-season games." He stopped as Dan reached out to snag a ball that the batter drove between him and the shortstop. Chris and Liz cheered, along with the other handful of people in the bleachers. Liz even waved Michelle's hands around.

As she shifted the baby to her other arm, she turned to Chris. "Would you be interested in taking on some music students? The high school band director sent a note out to all the teachers asking for referrals. Some students want to take private lessons."

He shook his head. "I wasn't a music ed major, so I don't know if they'd want me."

"He said they were desperate for brass instrument instructors — the professor at the college who had been working with most of the students left at the end of last year."

"Oh, Professor Yates." Chris nodded. "He's good. I took a few master classes with him when I first arrived on campus." He hesitated. "I guess I could apply." He reminded himself that it was music; better that than having to find a job in the campus food court. "I helped Katie with a piece a few weeks ago. It seemed to go OK, even though she plays French horn instead of trombone." He smiled. "She was worried about high school marching band auditions next week."

Liz disengaged the baby's fingers from her hair. "She'll be fine." She shook her head. "I don't know where Katie got the worry genes from — Dan and his sisters don't seem to have them, and Mikey's usually making the others worry with his stunts."

Chris couldn't help but laugh. "You should see what he pulled the other day." As he described the chaos when the youngest Reilly rewired the doorbells, he started to relax and settle into the rhythm of the game. Liz filled Chris in on the other Bulldogs and how Dan knew them. Most were old friends, guys who had grown up with Dan and Evan. He couldn't imagine being that close to anybody from that part of his life. He'd never quite fit in the rural town where he'd grown up and had been happy to escape when he left for college. It had been just a couple of counties over, but it'd been a chance to get out of that town, out of the house where his father ruled and his mother cringed. He shook off the memories and forced himself to concentrate on what Liz was saying. He didn't have to do much talking — just ask the occasional question. It carried them through the first few innings, which went quickly. The Bulldogs racked up the maximum number of runs allowed under the mercy rule each time at bat, and Chris lost track of how many times Dan had worked his way around the bases.

Other people watching the game would occasionally talk to Liz, but they left Chris alone, which was fine by him. The way Liz explained it, there would only be another inning, maybe two, before the mercy rule ended the game, and he was beginning to think he'd have to apologize to Dan for dragging his heels for no good reason. There'd only been that one incident with Joe before the game, and Chris didn't even know what had prompted that. Based on what Liz had said, run-ins between Dan and Joe were nothing new.

As Dan's team scored the tenth run of the inning and headed out to take the field, two little kids dashed over.

"Mrs. C!" The red-headed boy was covered in freckles. "My mom says you're going to be my teacher this year!" He turned to the smaller girl, who hid behind him. "Kara, you know Mrs. C."

She peeked out, her head framed in brown curls, and clung to the boy's T-shirt.

"Hi, Kara." Liz smiled, as the baby spit out the pacifier into the dirt and started to cry.

The boy made a face. "Ew! It's all dirty."

Liz fumbled in the diaper bag for a clean pacifier while trying to keep a hold on the squirming baby, and Chris held out his arms. "Here, let me take her. Colleen's always passing Sean or Pat over to me — she says I'm good with them."

Liz handed over the baby, and Chris let her gnaw on his knuckle, ignoring the game for the moment. A commotion on the field had him looking up to see Joe standing on third and Dan turning red.

"Oh, sh-" He stopped, remembering the three sets of little ears around him. "Liz." He jerked his head in the direction of the field. She looked and shook her head.

The boy looked over. "What's Dad saying to Mr. Dan?"

"Nothing, Tim." Liz kept her tone light, but Chris could see the tension in her shoulders. "Why don't you two go play on the swings with the other kids?" She pointed to a gated area closer to the school where six or seven other children were playing.

"But what about Dad?"

"Your dad's fine," she said. She rolled her shoulders, and Chris could see she was forcing herself to relax. It reminded him of his mother. Chris couldn't remember the first time he'd realized his mother always bit her lower lip right before she'd say something to try to shield him from his father's temper, but he had been older than Tim — 11? 12? He hoped Tim was still too young to realize Liz was about to shade the truth.

"You know how you and Robby sometimes fight about who gets the kickball first on the playground?" She looked at Tim, who nodded.

"He always wants to be first."

"But you and Robby are friends, right?"

Tim nodded. "So Dad and Mr. Dan are just arguing about who gets to be on third base?"

Liz nodded. "Come on, I'll walk you over to the playground."

Tim shook his head. "I'm a big boy. I don't need somebody to walk me over." He grabbed Kara's hand. "Come on, let's go."

Once the kids were gone, Chris looked back to the field. This wasn't two kids arguing over a playground ball. This was two adult men strong enough to do serious damage to each other if it became a physical confrontation. As strong as Dan was from hauling wood around all day, Joe had a good six inches on him. Trust Dan to get into it with somebody that much bigger than him without even flinching. Joe's face was red, and he sneered. Dan's face wasn't as easy to read, but his stance was clear. He'd take whatever Joe was planning to dish out. Chris wished he could be that sure of himself, but it was like muscle memory when he played — he just slipped into his old patterns of self-preservation.

He was beginning to regret not asking Liz if Joe was in fact the idiot Dan had mentioned before. Chris wished he could hear what they were saying, but since they were on the other side of the field, they would have to be yelling for that to happen. And he didn't want to hear that badly. There was no room for bleachers on that side — the Pirates fans were sitting on the stone wall behind the backstop — but some of the men in the dugout had walked over. The Bulldogs pitcher was holding the ball, looking over to third. Evan had started to come in from the outfield, but Dan waved him off. Dan stepped closer to Joe, who stepped back.

"Why isn't anybody doing anything?" Chris asked without looking at Liz.

She reached over and took Michelle back from him. "You saw Dan — he doesn't think he needs help. And Joe would never ask for any." She sighed. "I don't think anybody really wants to get into the middle of it anyway."

As she said that, the umpire stepped out from behind home plate and told the Bulldogs pitcher to start throwing. The men on the field turned back to the game, Dan included. Joe was still running his mouth as he stood a few feet down the third base line, waiting for a chance to score, but Dan seemed to be ignoring him. Chris felt the tension ease from his shoulders that the impending fight had been so easily defused.

Chris rubbed his hand over the scar on his arm. He was suddenly glad there was no alcohol allowed on school grounds, that the scent of stale beer was only in his head. He pressed his hand onto the warm bleacher, the ridged metal as far from chipped brick as possible.

"Chris?" He looked over to see Liz looking at him. "What's-"

Before she could ask, they heard the crack of a bat against a well-hit ball and looked back to see the neon ball flying back over Dan's head to where Evan roamed the outfield. It was deep, heading for the fence, and the runners were already moving, watching to see if it would drop. Joe had already run home and was standing on the plate, cheering. But as Evan reached the fence and jumped, he managed to snag the ball. He landed on the ground, rolling to come up to standing, ball still in his glove.

Liz cheered, clapping Michelle's hands together, as Evan fired the ball to Dan, the runners on the base paths scrambling back to avoid another out. Joe just stood on home plate, until one of the Pirates pushed him back toward third. He stumbled, then ran back, more elephant than gazelle. Dan's back was to him as he focused on the ball, his foot on the bag. The ball thwacked into Dan's glove, and he swept it back to tag Joe out. The man hadn't even tried to slide, and he pulled away from the tag. The ump jerked his fist to call Joe out, and Dan's team cheered, then headed back to the dugout.

Dan was up to bat first and made it to second base, standing up on a long hit to left center. Chris clapped and cheered with everybody else, smiling at the grin on Dan's face. The game settled back into the rhythm of every baseball game Chris had ever seen, not that he'd watched many. Dan's team scored more runs, moving runners around the bases.

"Joe's nasty, but it's all words."

"You're sure?" Chris' thumb traced the familiar path along his arm. "Dan doesn't back down."

Liz snickered. "Oh, believe me, I know. I'm usually the one arguing with him." She grinned. "We don't always agree, and we both love debating." Her smile faded. "I don't know what has you so worried, but Joe would never take a swing at him — or you."

Chris just looked at her.

"No, I'm serious." She set the baby in the carrier, the small eyes closing at once. "He'll yell, but he's not going to start a fist fight."

Chris rubbed his temples. "I don't know if I should be glad you're so confident or worried that you're sure because this happens regularly."

Liz put a hand on his shoulder. "I told you, we went to school together. I've known Dan forever — we're cousins of some kind, third or fourth. He and Evan have been best friends since Evan moved to town when we were in middle school — after everything that happened that summer, they were inseparable. And Joe was always around, one of the big kids."

"Point taken. You guys go way back." Chris rubbed the back of his neck, the tension resisting his attempts to massage it away. "Still, this isn't just your way of making me feel better, right? I thought you didn't like the idea of me coming tonight."

She shook her head, but waited to reply as they watched Evan make another spectacular catch in left field, ending the top of the fifth. As they sat back down, the cheers quieting, Liz said, "Dan won't back down from a fight — but he won't start one. And Joe won't throw a punch. He'll say a lot of idiotic stuff, but he won't lay a hand on Dan."

Chris nodded. "If you say so."

"The one time they did get in a fight, Dan kicked his ass. He was just a freshman, and Joe was a senior and captain of the football team." Liz smiled at the memory. "Nobody ever messed with Dan after that. Especially not Joe."

Chris nodded, his suspicion confirmed. "Dan mentioned that fight, but not that it was with Joe."

Before Chris could say anything else, Liz waved away some mosquitos buzzing around the baby carrier. "I'd better get her home before she gets eaten alive and I have a cranky pants on my hands all day tomorrow." She paused. "You OK? I can stay."

Chris shook his head. He still wasn't comfortable, but that wasn't Liz's problem. "I'm fine. Like you said, nothing's going to happen."

Liz nodded. "The mercy rule should kick in, and the game will be over in a few minutes anyway." She picked up the diaper bag and hung her purse on the stroller handle. "After this one, you guys should have fun celebrating at Corcoran's." Within minutes, she, the baby, and all their gear were gone, leaving Chris alone on his corner of the bleachers to watch the tail end of the game.

She was right, it didn't take long, the mercy rule kicking in once the Pirates failed to score. The Bulldogs didn't even get to bat again. As the teams lined up to shake hands, the people around Chris stood and gathered their stuff. He shoved his hands in his pockets and headed toward the dugout. Normally he didn't mind how affectionate Dan was — he'd gotten used to being hugged in public the first couple of weeks they'd dated — but this didn't seem like a good time. He walked behind the bench, figuring it might help to keep some distance.

Dan was at the end of the line, so Chris could see him high-fiving everybody on the other team — except Joe, who pulled his hand in, leaving Dan's to pass through empty air. Chris frowned, but it didn't seem like it was going to start a fight, so he tried to put it aside.

Evan greeted him. "I thought that was you sitting next to Liz."

Chris nodded. "Thanks for keeping her from knocking some sense into me — even though I needed it."

Before Evan could reply, Dan walked over, dropping his glove on the bench. "Good game to come to," he said. "We kicked ass tonight."

Another player walked over. "Corcoran's for beer to celebrate. You guys coming?"

Dan looked at Chris, who shrugged. Dan nodded. "We'll be there," he said.

"Was Michelle cranky when Liz left?" Evan looked at him.

"No, the bugs were biting." He scratched a spot on his shoulder. "She said to have fun celebrating."

Evan nodded, then grabbed the scorebook, as Dan hoisted the cooler.

They dropped the gear in Dan's truck, then crossed the Town Common to the Irish-style pub. Chris had never been inside — it was mostly a town hangout, not one the students frequented. He hadn't realized until the semester ended how many of Dan's favorite places weren't campus hangouts. After seeing Joe's reaction at the field, he wasn't sure this was the best idea, but nobody else seemed worried. Chris pushed aside his concerns and followed the others into the restaurant. Dan grabbed his hand and led him through the crowded room to the bar. Chris fought the urge to pull away.

"What'll it be?" The bartender looked up.

"Two drafts." Dan looked over his shoulder at Chris. "Wait, you did want beer?" At Chris' nod, Dan slid onto a stool, which tipped a bit. Dan let go of Chris' hand to steady himself on the bar, shifting around until the stool stopped rocking.

Chris grabbed the stool next to Dan, and Evan took the one on the other side of Dan.

"I think Liz told me everything about everybody. Not just them, but their parents and grandparents." Chris shook his head. "I can't imagine having all that information at my fingertips."

"Her family's been here as long as mine," Dan said. "Four generations. You just start to know these things."

"More than 10 years, and I still don't know a third of what she does," Evan said. "No wonder I barely passed the local history test Mrs. Kellen gave us in seventh grade."

The other two laughed, and Dan put his hand on Chris' shoulder to steady himself.

"The rest of us don't need to see that shit."

Chris froze; Dan's hand felt like a brand on his skin, marking the two of them.

"Joe, go away." Dan turned to look, sliding his arm around Chris' shoulders.

"It's a public bar, and I have as much right to be here as anybody." He didn't say anything else, and Chris didn't dare turn around. "You want to do that sort of thing, that's on you — but we shouldn't have to watch it."

Chris braced, waiting. Dan's arm was heavy across his shoulders, and Chris was torn between shrugging it off and leaning into it, hoping to draw strength from it. He took a deep breath and forced himself to turn and look at Joe. The man towered over Dan, his face a mask of disgust. Chris wanted to turn away, but he didn't want to give Joe the satisfaction.

"Problem here?" The bartender crossed his arms and lifted one eyebrow.

"No problem." Evan stood up, facing Joe. "He was just leaving. Right?"

Joe shook his head, but then Dan went to stand, and he backed away.

"Forget it." He walked away, muttering under his breath.

Chris swallowed, pressing his hands into his legs until they stopped shaking. "So, no problems with me coming to your game?" He frowned at Dan. "He looked like an awfully big problem to me."

"He's a bully." Dan shrugged. "Always has been. But he'd never do anything."

"That was nothing?" Chris shuddered. "We have very different ideas of what 'anything' means." He started to say more, but stopped. Now was not the time.

"Dan's right. He wouldn't do anything." The bartender slid three pints of beer across the scarred wood. "You guys want me to let the chief know about this, just in case?"

Dan shook his head. "What's he going to do? Joe would have to touch one of us to hurt us, and that's not going to happen."

Chris shook his head. "You guys seem awfully sure you can predict how he's going to react."

"He normally won't get within five feet of me." Dan rolled his eyes. "He's ruined enough of the night — let's just drop it." He grabbed his beer, and the three men headed over to where the rest of the team was gathered. An hour and three beers each later, Dan and Chris headed out.

"You're not picking up the truck now, not after that many drinks," Chris said as they winced at the blast of heat outside, despite the darkness.

"Tomorrow," Dan said. "Your place or mine?"

"Mine."

Dan shook his head. "I've been telling you that you don't have to sneak out — you can stay at my place."

Chris opened his mouth, and Dan held up a hand. "I know, I know." Dan rolled his eyes again. "Come on." But when he turned down the alley between two buildings, Chris stopped.

Dan looked back. "I thought you wanted to go to your place."

"I do."

"If we cut down here, it'll shave three blocks off the walk."

Chris hesitated. Dan wouldn't suggest this shortcut if he knew about that night, but since Chris had never told him... "OK." He swallowed and made himself take a step into the alley. The trash bins along the wall smelled of stale beer, and bile started to rise in his throat. He forced himself to take another step, reminding himself the wall was cinderblock, not brick. A third step. It wasn't nearly as late, the sky still the blue of dusk, not the black of night. He started to take another step, but a noise stopped him; he looked back for the source. A couple of the Bulldogs walked by the entrance to the alley, and he let out his breath.

"You OK?" Dan's hand on his back was firm, reassuring.

"Ask me that when we get home." He breathed through his mouth, trying to avoid the odor that brought back memories and forced himself to walk as quickly as he could to get through the alley to the open street beyond. From there, it was only another block to his apartment in one of the old Victorian homes that had been divided into smaller spaces to meet the needs of college students.

Inside, he dropped down on the old couch he'd picked up at a secondhand store for $10. He was glad he hadn't been able to afford to buy new — it was the most comfortable piece of furniture he'd ever owned. He settled into the cushions, their softness cradling him and making him feel safe. "Sure, go to your game. Nobody's going to say anything. Nobody will mind." He didn't bother to squash down his sarcasm. Dan wouldn't mind. For all Liz said about being glad Dan could be himself around Chris, Chris knew it went both ways. He dropped his head back and squeezed his eyes shut. Arms folded, he ran his thumb over the scar, the smell of stale beer and feel of rough brick still in his head. "You didn't mention the high school idiot was still around."

He felt the cushions shift as Dan sat next to him. He waited for the hand or arm around his shoulders, but it never came. Chris couldn't tell if Dan was just giving him space or if he had just screwed up badly enough to override Dan's usual need for physical contact. Sighing, he shook his head. "Look, I'm sorry I waited this long to come, but do you see why?" His fingers traced the line of memories.

"He's one idiot, not worth mentioning." Dan paused, then his calloused fingers stopped Chris' hand as it ghosted over the scar on his other arm. "You finally going to tell me about this?"

Chris sighed. "I should have done it before tonight, so you'd understood what you were asking." He kept his eyes closed as he made himself face the memory. He didn't want to talk about it, didn't want to relive that night. But Dan needed to know. "It was a summer night, a lot like this one."

He paused, ordering his thoughts. "It was three summers ago, right before my senior year of undergrad. I stayed in town that summer to get some of my theory and history classes out of the way." Chris let his fingers trace the scar. "It meant I would be able to perform in more ensembles during the year. Back then, all I wanted to do was play. It wasn't just the performance. There was one guy, a trumpet player, who just liked performing. It didn't matter what he was doing — music, theater — he got a rush from the spotlight." He shook his head. "I don't care about the performance, not really. I feed off the music, how it feels when I create it. It's better with an audience because their reaction becomes part of the experience, but I'd be happy playing even without anybody around."

"But-"

Chris shook his head, and Dan stopped. Chris hunted for the words to explain. "From the first time I picked up an instrument back in middle school, I knew I'd found what I wanted to do. So I had studied and practiced and had a lot of experience and just wanted to play as much as I could my senior year, between campus groups and a quintet I'd joined a year earlier. Those guys were home for the summer, so I picked up some gigs here and there as a sub, waited tables to pay the bills." He swallowed. "Like here, I was out on campus, had been for a year or two." He hesitated. "But that was it. This was one of the smaller state schools. There weren't many people from my hometown there, and I didn't see them much around campus. That's the way I wanted it. My family didn't know — my father assumed but, as long as I didn't say anything, all he would do was call me names."

"Why didn't you leave the state, find some place further away?" Dan still wasn't touching him, but he had moved closer. "You could have come up here."

Chris shook his head. "Jazz musicians don't exactly rake in the money. My father wasn't going to pay for me to major in music, and I didn't want to have any debt when I graduated. By staying in state and working my ass off to get good grades and do work-study, I didn't have to take out loans."

"So what happened that summer?"

Chris rubbed the back of his neck, wishing he could skip this part. "I was careful off campus, didn't want people to know I was gay. Like you said, rural Virginia is more conservative than here. That summer, I wasn't dating anybody, so it was easy to keep it quiet. I didn't have time even for casual, not as much as I was working." He shook his head. "One night, an ex came into the restaurant. He was drinking, and he got loud. Tried to convince me to get back together with him."

"And when you didn't want to, he got mad." Dan ran his hand up Chris' arm, sliding it across his shoulders.

Chris shook his head. "It wasn't the dating — I just didn't want to have the conversation there. I figured out pretty quickly that if word got out I was gay, a couple of my coworkers would be more than happy to kick my ass. And I'd heard a few stories about the sheriff's deputies — I didn't want to take my chance with them." He pinched the bridge of his nose. "Nothing happened — then."

"Then?"

Chris nodded. "After closing, I headed out the back door, cutting through the alleys to get home." He heard Dan draw in a breath. "Yeah. A couple of guys from the kitchen were lying in wait, attacked as soon as I got close." He couldn't tell Dan all of it, how they pressed him into the brick wall by the trash bins, the stench of unwashed bottles thick enough to clog his breath, the rough wall scraping his cheek and forehead until he could feel blood trickling down his face. Each blow drove him against the unyielding wall, making him worry they would damage his hands, his ability to play. His dream. The abuse they heaped upon him — he tried to block out the words, to figure out how to get out of this before they did permanent damage. But he skipped that, only saying, "You spend most of your time playing big brass instruments, you get pretty strong. I managed to shake them off, but one of them had a knife." He resisted the urge to trace the scar again. "Sliced me deep, through a couple of layers of muscle."

"How did you get away?"

He snorted. "The blood scared them — one of them started yelling about AIDS, and they ran." He shook his head. "If they hadn't been so ignorant, they might have killed me. I didn't stand much of a chance against that knife." He swallowed. "31 stitches. It did so much damage, I couldn't play until after Halloween." He pressed his hand to his arm the way he had that night, trying to stop the bleeding. "I had to change all my classes, do physical therapy until winter break. It was so close to my elbow, it nicked a couple of tendons. At first they thought I wouldn't ever be able to fully straighten my arm again."

"Shit." Dan pulled him close, his arms wrapping tight. "Without that... You wouldn't be able to play."

Chris shook his head, knowing Dan would feel it even if he couldn't see because he had Chris so close. "That's why I switched to composing. It was the only music degree I could still finish on time, and I didn't want to stay there any longer than I had to." He absorbed strength from Dan's arms, enough to keep going. "I had a lot of time to think that year, since I couldn't play for the first semester. One of my professors suggested I think about teaching and was willing to write a good recommendation for grad school."

"Do you ever think about changing back to performing?" Dan's voice was muffled against his neck.

Chris thought about how to explain. "For a living? No. Even now, three years later, I still can feel where the knife sliced my arm after I play for a few hours. The muscles would get stronger if I was playing as much as I'd need to when performing, but I don't know if it would be enough."

Dan pulled back a bit and looked at him. After studying his face, Dan said, "You said it wasn't the spotlight for you, it was the music. And you can still play."

Chris nodded, glad Dan understood. "I've learned to be happy with what I do have — I can't go back and not walk down that alley.

Dan pulled him close again. "No wonder you didn't... I'm sorry. I shouldn't have pushed."

Chris was comforted by the strength in Dan's arms, something he only relaxed enough to enjoy when they were alone. "It was my choice. And your family's been great. Evan, Liz... Anybody in the bleachers tonight could tell I was dating you if they had bothered to listen to Liz and me talking." He opened his eyes for the first time. "Nobody said anything."

"And they were definitely listening." Dan grinned. "They might not have said anything, but they were listening."

"You and Joe have a history."

Dan nodded. "Having to admit the 'freshman fag' beat up the captain of the football team pretty much guaranteed he was going to hate me for life. But he's the one who started it." He shrugged. "He's the only one who's ever really given me a hard time, and he's a bully. He'll back down if you get in his face."

"Because that's really my style." Chris rolled his eyes.

Dan laughed and just like that, the mood was broken. They shifted away from the heavy stuff for tonight. When they finally went to sleep, Chris settled in, Dan spooned against his back like always.

Chris lay on the ground, his arm dripping blood on the black slacks he wore for work. He wiped his other hand on his pants and pressed it to his arm to try to stop the bleeding from the gaping wound. A few people would still be at the restaurant, but he wasn't going back in there. Not now, not after this. He swallowed and tried to sit up, his stomach churning. He had to lean against the wall, gritting his teeth, as he fought the urge to puke.

When he felt less queasy, he tried to get up, but couldn't without taking his hand off the slice in his arm. He took a deep breath, then pushed himself up as quickly as possible, swaying at the rapid change. Once up, he wiped the gravel from his hand and pressed it back against the cut. It was two blocks to the police station. He didn't know if they would help, not once they found out why he ended up like this, but he didn't have much choice.

Chris woke up panting and sweaty, realizing he hadn't shut it away.

"You with me?" Dan lay next to him, the moon casting just enough light for Chris to see his face.

He nodded. "Yeah. Nightmare."

"I figured that when you started struggling and shouting." Dan paused. "You get these a lot?"

"Not since I left Virginia." He shivered as the sweat cooled. Dan got up and came back with a damp washcloth and towel. Chris took them both and cleaned up, tossing them on the chair under the window. "I'll be fine — just haven't made myself remember all the details in a long time." He lay back down. Dan waited a second, then joined him, pulling the sheet over them. He opened his mouth, and Chris held up a hand. "You've got a job in the morning, and I have a meeting with my advisor about my thesis. We can talk about it later."

But he couldn't fall asleep. He felt Dan's arms around him and tried to relax, but every time he closed his eyes, he was back in that alley.

The next morning, Chris tried not to yawn in his advisor's face. As soon as they were finished, he went to the student lounge. With a week to go before the semester started, the room was empty, and he thought about taking a nap on the ragged couch. Instead, he grabbed a mug of coffee, but the first sip made him grimace.

"I've got paint thinner that isn't as strong as that miscrable excuse for coffee." Professor Stone — Becca — dumped an armful of books on the desk by the door and shoved her hair back behind her ear, only to have it flop back out. "At least it has some bite, though. I'm stealing some — the dean's secretary might as well be making colored dishwater for all the flavor the coffee in the faculty offices has." She poured a mug, flopped into the chair with holes at the corners of the arms, and kicked off her sandals. "You look like you got run over. Late night?" She wiggled her eyebrows above her red- and purple-striped glasses.

Chris shook his head. "Not that kind of a late night." He set the mug on the scarred table and slumped back. "Just one of those nasty moments that comes back and smacks you around." He rubbed his arm, wishing he could somehow erase the mark and the memories. "You have any of those, Professor?"

"Becca," she chided. "I've got my share." She drained her mug and set it down. "Yours have anything to do with what happened at Corcoran's after the softball game?"

Chris just stared. "What the-"

"Word gets around."

"I'll bet." Chris rubbed the back of his neck. "That's what I get for listening when Dan said I should come to his game. Sure, no big. Nobody's going to care his boyfriend is there. Nobody would say anything." He snorted. "Yeah, right. That's the last ballgame I go to."

"So you're going to let that O'Leary idiot scare you away?" She shook her head. "I don't care how nasty that old moment was, you can't let it dictate your life. And you're not skipping my cookout. That boy's not invited, and I'm not letting you back out."

"It's not that easy."

"It doesn't have to be as hard as you're making it either." She folded her legs under her and softened her tone. "I know all about what happened in Virginia."

"I just told Dan last night." Chris jerked upright. "How did you find out already?"

"I knew a year ago." Becca sipped her coffee. "The admin weenies roped me into being on the grad school admissions committee last year. Most of the applications are easy to sort into the Yes or No pile, but we always have a handful that the whole committee reviews. Yours was one of them." She paused. "I had a friend in the art department at your school, so I called to ask her who in music I could talk to. Turns out I didn't need to. She knew why you had switched specialties so late, gave me all the details."

Chris let his head drop back and looked up at the ceiling. "So everybody knows?"

"They know you were injured and couldn't perform," she said. "I didn't share the details. That wasn't any of their business."

"It wasn't yours, either." He winced when he realized he'd said that out loud.

Becca chuckled. "No, it wasn't. But I didn't share the information — with anybody — and it got you here."

"I guess." Chris sighed and looked over at her.

"None of that." Becca sat up. "You didn't let those ignoramuses who attacked you stop you then; don't start now. If you want something, you fight for it, just the way you did then."

"For the right to go to Dan's softball games?" He shook his head.

"It's not just the games." She sighed. "I must have heard from a dozen people this morning that they'd finally met you last night."

He frowned. "I only met Liz."

"She might be the only one you talked to, but lots of people noticed you were there."

He dropped his head into his hands. "Great. So much for under the radar."

"Chris." Her hand touched his shoulder, just for a minute, then dropped. "It's not a bad thing. We know Dan. We know his family. We know he's been happy since you two started dating, and the Reillys like you."

He sighed. "Right. Small town." He massaged his temples, trying to stave off the headache brewing behind his eyes. "I wasn't going to deal with this again. Just come here, get my degree, and move to a big city with lots of opportunities where this wouldn't be an issue."

"One man. One idiot. You're willing to run from one of the best guys you'll ever know over that?" Becca crossed her arms.

"One idiot yesterday. How many more tomorrow?" He squeezed his eyes shut. "What happens when it's somebody Dan respects?"

"The only person who had an issue with Dan — over anything — is that O'Leary boy, and he's got other problems." Becca got up to refill her mug. "Dan's never been ashamed of who he is, never tried to hide it."

He couldn't think how to explain that was half the problem. Dan didn't — couldn't — know. Dan was the only man he'd ever dated who hadn't spent years hiding. He envied that and still didn't understand how Dan was that comfortable in his own skin. He settled for the easier answer. "Dan's related to half the town. I'm not." It felt like a percussion solo in his head now. "They might be fine with him. Doesn't mean they're fine with me." He pressed his fingers into the smooth ridge, remembering. "I'm not going to do this again."

"So you're going to run." Becca huffed out a breath. "I thought you had more backbone than that."

"I can't stay. Not if it means going through this again."

"And where are you going to run to?" she asked. "Every place has morons who will judge you against their own small-minded standards. If you run now, you'll always be running. Some people aren't going to like you. It doesn't matter who you are. You going to let a bunch of people who don't respect you determine how you live your life?" She shook her head. "Hell of a life. Why even bother?"

He didn't have an answer for her, and she didn't stay long enough for him to find one right then. Chris gave up and dumped the last of the coffee down the drain, then grabbed his backpack and headed home. Enough. When he got back to his place, he pulled out his trombone and his practice mute and sat down in front of his music stand. At first he was just playing, not even looking at the arrangement in front of him. After a while, he stopped and massaged his arm where the muscles had tightened. His head was clearer, and he honed in on the new piece he'd been writing.

By the time he finished working out the melody line, his lack of sleep was catching up to him. Yawning, he headed for the bedroom. He was so tired, he didn't notice the crisp paper bag on his nightstand until he went to set down his watch. Chris replaced the bag with the watch, then reached inside, wondering where it had come from. He pulled out a CD case and flipped it over to find the new Glenn Ferris album on his list to buy the next time he had some extra money. He squinted at the sticky note on it, trying to decipher Dan's scribble.

I'm sorry. I wouldn't have asked if I'd known. Mind some company to listen to this after tonight's game? We've got the early one — done by 8. I'll bring dinner. — D

Chris smiled and put the CD back on the nightstand. He'd wait to listen to it until tonight. He lay down and pulled the sheet over him, quickly falling to asleep. There were no nightmares this time. When he woke, the afternoon sun was low, shining right on his face. He fumbled for his watch. Just past 5. He stretched and sat up. The CD with Dan's note was sitting on the nightstand. Chris went to pull it off, then hesitated. Tonight's game wasn't against the Pirates, and everybody insisted Joe was the only person who might be an issue. So if he went tonight, Joe wouldn't be there. They weren't going to Corcoran's after — they were coming back here to listen to music. It wouldn't be the same. And he couldn't argue with Becca — letting Joe determine his life was even more stupid than the man's attitude toward him and Dan.

But half an hour later, as he approached the ball field again, he hesitated. Dan wasn't expecting him. After last night, he wouldn't. But if they were going to make this work, if this was going to last, Chris had to do this for himself as well as for them as a couple. He forced himself to walk through the gate.

He recognized some faces from last night. A few exchanged greetings, and Chris felt a little tension slip from his shoulders. He took the same seat in the bleachers, still wary. Liz wasn't there, but he still managed to enjoy watching Dan and his friends play. This game wasn't like last night's blowout — the Bulldogs were behind by five going into the bottom of the ninth. When Evan knocked in a bases-clearing home run, Chris jumped to his feet with the rest of them. The teams for the next game were starting to arrive, and everybody stopped to watch the ball sail through the sky over the center field fence. When Chris dropped back in his seat, he knocked his water bottle to the ground. He bent over to pick it up, just as a cleat-clad foot kicked it away.

He looked up to see Joe standing there, and the protest forming on his lips died.

Chris forced his lungs to suck in another breath and turned his back on Joe.

"What, you don't want it? Or do you want to leave your germs around so everybody else can catch it?" Joe's voice was low, and Chris had to focus on his breathing. He was not going to panic, and he was not going to argue. He was going to keep his head down, not attract attention, the way he always did. He was going to watch Dan try to hit the ball.

"You afraid of me, boy?" Joe paused, and Chris fought the urge to turn around. "Worried that a real man would leave you in a bloody pulp?"

Stale beer. Rough brick. The end of his performing dream. And the start of a new path. One he wasn't going to run from just because that would be easier.

"Stupid fa-"

Chris turned around, focused on keeping his voice even. "You really want to start this here? Now?"

"Start what?" Joe held up his hands. "I'm just standing here."

"Like you were just trying to get a beer last night, right?" He forced himself to stand. They were the same height, and he deliberately faced Joe. "The way I hear it, you've been fighting this same fight for almost 10 years and you haven't won once. You want to keep beating your head against the wall, go for it. No matter how many insults you throw at us, we're always going to be who we are. You're not going to change us."

Joe stepped back. "Like I want to have anything to do with a pair of queers." Before Joe could say anything else, the crack of a bat split the air. Chris turned around to see the ball headed deep into the outfield, Dan racing around the bases almost on the heels of the runner who had been on first. "Come on, come on!" The crowd chanted as they watched the ball drop just behind the fielder, who snagged it, rocketing it back to the cutoff man, who turned and fired for home. Dan put on a burst of speed and slid into home, sending the rest of the team pouring out of the dugout onto the field.

Chris put Joe out of his mind. He smiled and headed over to the dugout as the other team trudged off the field. Half of his uniform was covered in dirt, and Dan was grinning as the rest of the Bulldogs slapped him on the back and high-fived him for his walk-off home run. He made his way through his teammates to where Chris was standing.

"You came." Dan's grin widened to a huge smile as he grabbed his glove from the end of the bench.

Chris nodded and smiled. "I did." And when Dan reached out and pulled him into a hug, Chris let him.

JENNIE COUGHLIN

END RUN

October 2006

F.X. O'Leary was in the back of the store sweeping when he heard the jingle of someone opening the front door. He stepped around the corner and looked, but couldn't see anyone over the rows of shelves. Frowning, he checked his watch. The middle school and high school wouldn't be out for another 20 minutes. He brushed the dust into the pan, then dumped it into the bin in the stockroom. He quieted his footsteps as he walked toward the front, looking for whomever had entered the store.

All he found was a blue canvas backpack behind the counter. He checked the time again. Still too early for Tim to be out of school, so what was his grandson's backpack doing here? And where was Tim?

O'Leary picked up the bag and noticed a rip in one corner and some dirt on the front. It was only the third week of school, and the backpack was a sturdy one. Mary had insisted on it over Joe's objections when she took the grandchildren school shopping last month. O'Leary shook his head. Honestly, his son just lacked sense sometimes. He wanted the kids to have those silly character book bags, thought they were cool. No consideration for the cheap materials they were made of or how they would be in pieces within weeks and need replacing. Mary had chosen these because they would wear well. That rip couldn't have come from snagging it on a locker.

Before F.X. could find Tim, some customers walked in. Newcomers, not anybody he knew more than in passing, so he had to wait until they left. Except by then, school was out, and the kids piled in with crumpled dollar bills and handfuls of change to get a bottle of tonic, a bag of chips, or a candy bar before heading home. He made a mental note of a couple of them so he could say something the next time their parents stopped in. Bill McMasters didn't need four candy bars, not when he'd bought three yesterday. His mother usually stopped in for a gallon of milk or a loaf of bread on her way home from work. He'd mention it to her then.

It was almost four o'clock when the store quieted down enough for him to start looking for Tim. He called his wife first, just to make sure Tim hadn't gone to the house. Kara was there, but Mary didn't mention Tim. He didn't ask if she'd seen him, not wanting her to worry.

When he walked back into the stockroom, he could see the glow of a light in the back. He found Tim there, flashlight in hand, reading one of his Harry Potter books. His face was smudged with dirt, and his jeans were ripped in the knees.

"Tim."

The boy curled up for a second before looking up. "Grandpa?"

"What are you doing back here in the dark? You usually do your homework at my desk behind the counter." He reached a hand down and noted when Tim hesitated before taking it. When the 12-year-old stood, he was almost as tall as F.X., and the older man added another note to his mental list to have Mary figure out if his grandson needed new clothes. "Tim?"

"It's quiet back here." He shrugged and turned away. "Do you need me to help with something, or should I go to see Nana and do my homework?"

"You can do your homework here." He wanted to keep an eye on the boy. Something wasn't right.

"It's too noisy here." Tim hunched his shoulders, his T-shirt hanging off his skinny frame. "I'll go to your house until Dad comes to get us." He kept his back to F.X. and headed into the store. Before F.X. could stop him, Tim was gone, backpack slung over one shoulder as he disappeared out the door.

He intended to talk to his son about his concerns when Joe picked the children up that evening, but by the time he closed up the store, they had already left.

F.X. held his tongue through dinner, debating what he should do.

"Franny, what is your problem?" Mary stood at the sink washing their plates. "You haven't told a single story about your day. That's not like you." She set the plate in the drying rack.

"I've a lot on my mind." He hoped that would be enough, but he should have known better.

"Does this have anything to do with the children?" She looked over her shoulder to where he sat at the kitchen table.

"Why do you say that?"

"Don't get cute with me, Francis Xavier." She turned back to the sink. "I've known you since we were six. I know when you're avoiding something."

"Why do you assume it has to do with the children?" He got up and got a bottle of beer from the refrigerator.

Mary shook her head. "Kara's been too quiet lately, and Tim is scared of his own shadow. That's not like our boy."

"No, it's not." He hesitated, then told her about that afternoon. "I think he got into a fight."

"That's not like him, either." She hung the dishtowel over the oven handle to dry. "Joe got into fights in high school, but Tim never has."

"Joe started fights," F.X. corrected her. "I don't think Tim started this one."

"I should talk to Joe about it." Mary nodded, then started wiping down the table. "He can talk to the principal."

"He's more likely to try and teach Tim how to fight back." F.X. sighed. "Do you think Kara knows?"

"I don't know." Mary rinsed off the sponge. "Have you heard from Annabelle?"

F.X. shook his head. "It's been six months since her last letter. I wish I knew how to track her down. I know she was afraid she wouldn't be able to break free of Joe if she took the children, but they need her."

Mary settled down at the kitchen table, folding her hands. "Maybe you should talk to Fr. Morelli. He knows Joe well, and Joe would listen to him."

He shook his head. "A couple of parents of Kara's classmates have been in the store this week complaining that he told them their girls couldn't sign up to be altar servers unless they didn't have enough boys sign up to replace the high school students who left for college." He massaged his temples. "Has Kara mentioned wanting to be an altar server?"

"No, but she asked if I could take her to children's choir rehearsals on Wednesdays. Colleen McDonald's been trying to recruit more children to join. I asked Joe, and he said as long as it was for the church, she could definitely participate." Mary paused. "When I pick her up from CCD — sorry, religious education — tomorrow, I can talk with some of the mothers, see if they know anything."

F.X. turned the idea over in his head. "No, you'd better not. Annabelle only left because we were here to keep an eye on the children. She's always known that Joe and I don't see eye to eye in a lot of areas, and she told me she was counting on me to keep him from getting so conservative he would suffocate the children the way he was doing to her. If Joe gets mad at both of us, I'm not sure where that leaves them. We'd best keep you out of this so he feels like he can still send them over here after school." He drained the last of his beer, then examined the bottle. "I don't wish Joe was drinking again, but I'm afraid he's going too far in the other direction. He's thrown himself so far into the Church, and into the most conservative parts of it, that I worry he's trying to force the children to be people they aren't."

He wasn't surprised that Mary ignored that comment — she never did like to criticize the Church — instead saying, "Why don't you talk to Liz Czarnecki next time she stops in the store? She's Kara's teacher this year, and she had Tim. She might have an idea."

F.X. agreed and waited for the teacher to come by the shop. Liz stopped in two days later to pick up a gallon of milk on her way home, and he asked the question.

She frowned as she ran a hand through her untidy curls. "I don't think I can answer that." She hesitated. "Joe never named you and Mrs. O as guardians for Kara, which means there are a lot of things I can't discuss with you."

"Even though we care for her and Tim every day?" F.X. leaned on the counter. "When Annabelle left, she made us promise to look after the children, to let her know if she ever needed to come back for them. She knew Joe would cut off her mother, but she figured we'd still be part of their lives."

"Have you contacted her?" Liz set her purse down on the counter. "She's their mother. I could talk to her. Unless Joe terminated her parental rights, but you would know about that. The judge wouldn't do that without a hearing, and since you see Joe and the children almost every day, they would have probably called you as witnesses."

F.X. hesitated for a minute. "She stayed in touch with me. Annabelle might have stayed in touch with her mother, too — the one time I called over, she hung up before I could ask. I told Annabelle that the next time I called, and she said not to call her mother again; it wouldn't go well. Since then, every four to six weeks, Annabelle would send a letter with an update and give me an address where I could reply with news about the children. It was different each time. She gave me a phone number last year, said it was a cell phone so even if Joe found it, he wouldn't be able to find her. She said if there was ever an emergency, she wanted me to be able to reach her." He sighed. "I haven't heard from her in six months, and when I called the number this week, it was disconnected. I tried calling Annabelle's mother, but she's moved. And I couldn't find a new number for her."

"I would talk to Riordan," Liz said.

"Talk to me about what?"

F.X. looked over to see his old friend in the market doorway. "Well, it's complicated."

Riordan smiled. "I'm a lawyer — we make everything complicated."

F.X. filled Riordan in. After he was done, the lawyer turned to Liz.

"Have you seen anything?"

Liz shook her head. "You know I'm required by law to report any signs of abuse — physical or otherwise." She turned to F.X. "All teachers are." She paused. "I have not made any reports like that this school year, and I haven't seen anything that makes me think I need to make one. I'll keep a close eye out for the rest of the year."

F.X. nodded. "That eases my mind a bit." He massaged his temples. "Do you know any of the middle school teachers? I would feel better if I knew everything was all right with Tim."

Liz nodded. "I know a couple of them. I can mention it." She checked her watch. "Right now, I have to get home, or Michelle won't have time to eat before soccer practice." She headed out, and F.X. looked around. Nobody else was in the small store.

"So, can you help me?" He looked at Riordan, who nodded and stepped behind the counter, pulling out a stool.

"If anybody comes in, I'll start telling a story."

F.X. stepped behind the deli counter and pulled out one of the tonic cans he kept there. "Have a Coke." He smiled. "Can't tell stories without something to wet you down."

Riordan grinned. "Good thinking." He popped the top and set it on the counter. "Liz is right, unfortunately. She can't talk to you or Mary, not until paperwork is filed with the school. The same is true of Tim's teachers, their doctors, pretty much anybody who might be able to help the kids or report evidence that they need help to the authorities."

F.X. sighed. "It doesn't seem fair."

Riordan nodded. "No, it doesn't. Joe might have you two doing many of the things a parent would, but without the legal documentation, you both are barred from many things. If you had to take one of them to the ER, you couldn't consent to treatment either." He frowned. "And there's been no word from Annabelle?"

F.X. shook his head. "I've written to her at the last address twice now, with no response." He dug the scrap of paper out from the drawer where he'd hidden it away.

Riordan noted it, then paused. "Would she come back?"

F.X. hesitated. "I have to hope so." He thought back. "I'm still not sure of everything that happened between them. She stuck by him when he was drinking, stayed after he came back to the Church and stopped. But she once said she didn't know what was worse — Joe drunk or Joe sober."

"But when she left, she didn't take Tim and Kara." Riordan folded his hands. "That's not going to help things, even if we can get her to come back."

"She said she didn't dare." F.X. shook his head. "Joe wouldn't consider the idea of divorce, and that one lawyer had been making such a fuss around the state about father's rights the past few years, she was afraid trying to file without his agreement would put them through hell." He stood and started pacing. "Mary and I talked a couple of nights ago, and she's staying away from this. If he gets mad at me, I want him to feel like he can still send them to the house with her after school."

Riordan frowned, but when the market door opened, he switched gears. "So then the judge told me-" He broke off. "Hey there, Chris."

The blond man smiled and greeted the older men. "I hate to break up storytime, but I need to get some ham, roast beef, and cheese." He shook his head. "Dan planned to stop by, but he and his dad got held up on a job. It was either this or peanut butter and jelly for dinner."

F.X. laughed as he got the cold cuts from the display case and started slicing. "Don't tell me neither of you boys has learned how to cook after all these years."

"Oh, Eileen taught all of them how to cook," Chris said. "Mike's better than half his sisters. But the softball team did better in the weekend tournament than Dan expected, and we never got to the grocery store."

F.X. chatted away as he sliced meat and cheese, forcing himself to be patient. The store was as much information center as food supplier. If he didn't spend some time catching up with the friends and neighbors who came in, they would wonder and ask questions. Before long, he was ringing up Chris' order and bagging the cold cuts.

"Have a good night," Chris said. "Riordan, if Becca's dragging you to the faculty social Saturday, we'll catch up with you then. You two are the best way to keep the rest of us from dying of boredom."

F.X. shook his head as Chris left. "That boy was so quiet when he first got here." He sighed as he washed his hands. "Reminded me then of Tim now — withdrawn, timid." He sat down heavily. "Tim's never been a social butterfly, but ever since he started school this year, it's like he's trying to disappear into himself."

"And he won't talk about it?"

F.X. shook his head. "He'll be here tomorrow after school, because Mary has to take Kara to the dentist. I can try to find out more then."

Riordan tipped his head to one side and quirked his lips. "Will Tim be here all afternoon?"

F.X. nodded. "Mary and Kara won't get home much before five o'clock, so it wouldn't be worth sending him over there. When this kind of thing happens, Joe usually just stops by here to pick him up."

Riordan paused, thinking. "That could work." He took a deep breath. "Let me think on it. Now, back to what you were saying before, about leaving Mary out of this."

"We talked a couple of nights ago." F.X. leaned an elbow on the counter. "She's as worried as I am, but I thinks it's better that Joe not know she's involved."

Riordan nodded. "That rules out any sort of fight in court. We could petition for you both to get custody of them if it seems like Tim and Kara would come to actual harm staying with Joe, but if it doesn't work, he could block you out completely. And not all judges will consider that ruling, especially without clear evidence of abuse."

"Which we don't have." F.X. sighed. "I don't want to think my boy's a bad father." He hesitated. "I know he's got his faults and his blind spots. I often don't understand him, but..."

Riordan nodded. "I know. Look, I have some ideas. I'll be by tomorrow. Just follow my lead."

F.X. couldn't help worrying. "You're not exactly Joe's favorite person, you know."

"I'm no more liberal than you are, but he just doesn't have to accept me. He can't disown his own father. Besides, I don't need him to like me to do an end run around him." Riordan smiled. "If this doesn't work, I'll find another solution. But I think I can finagle it."

F.X. chuckled. "That is what you do best."

The next afternoon, F.X. kept an ear out for Tim if he had to be away from the front of the store. The boy showed up just minutes after school let out. He must have come straight over, another worrying sign. He should be horsing around with his classmates — taking twice as long to get anywhere and taking up the entire sidewalk in the process.

"Hey, Grandpa." He dropped his backpack in its usual spot.

"You have much homework today?" F.X. glanced over, but kept shelving soup cans, not wanting to spook Tim.

"Not much." The boy pulled out the same Harry Potter book from the other day. "I'm going out back to read. It's quieter there." He didn't wait for an answer, just disappeared into the storeroom. F.X. let him go and thought about what he'd seen. A black mark, like grease, on the shoulder of Tim's shirt. No obvious bruises or scrapes, but if he was being bullied, the kids might be smart enough not to mark him up where a teacher might notice.

He didn't have time to think any more about it because the after-school rush started. Some of the last kids to come to the counter were Jason and Matt, two boys Tim had been friends with for years.

"Hey, Mr. O!" Jason grinned as he put a can of root beer and two small bags of potato chips on the counter.

F.X. looked at the food, then at the boy. "Your mom know you're spoiling your dinner like that?"

"Mr. O, I'm starving!" He nodded so hard his brown hair fell across his face, and he shoved it back. "Lunch was hours and hours ago."

F.X. shook his head. "I swear, you boys act like you've got a tapeworm sometimes. Tim's grandma swears he has a hollow leg."

Jason just shrugged and held out three crumpled dollar bills.

F.X. took them and wondered. He tossed out another comment while he was making change. "Haven't seen you boys around much lately."

Neither Jason nor Matt said anything, just took the snacks and dashed out.

F.X. sighed. No wonder Tim was retreating into books, if his oldest friends didn't want to hang out with him.

As the afternoon wore on, he wondered again what Riordan had up his sleeve. Once the clock hit quarter of five, the minutes seemed to drag. The store was quiet, so he headed back to the storeroom.

"Tim?" He looked around and saw his grandson sitting in the corner, the thick book open on his lap. "Your dad's going to be here soon." He frowned as Tim seemed to shrink into himself. "Come on, join me out front."

"In a minute, Grandpa." Tim didn't look up. "I just want to finish this chapter."

F.X. nodded and left the boy where he was. Might be for the best anyway since he didn't know what scheme Riordan had dreamed up.

He didn't have to wait much longer. Joe walked in just past five, and Riordan was only a minute behind him.

"Do you have any of that roast beef left?" Riordan walked over to the deli counter. "Oh, sorry, Joe." He turned to face the younger man, who was leaning on the counter. "I didn't mean to interrupt you and your dad."

"Boy's still not ready." Joe snorted. "Got his nose in some damn book again."

"Joseph." F.X. glared over the top of the deli counter. He hoped this didn't mean Joe was in a mood to argue, or Riordan wouldn't be able to get him to agree to anything. Honestly, no wonder Annabelle couldn't stand to live with him anymore.

Joe rolled his eyes. "Fine, some book." He shook his head. "He can't remember simple basketball rules at CYO team tryouts, but he'll spout off obscure facts from a book that weighs more than he does."

"Tim's playing CYO ball this year?" Riordan's voice was casual. "Father Morelli mentioned tryouts were this weekend when he asked me about the forms yesterday."

"Forms?" F.X. didn't have to act to sound puzzled.

"Yes, the bishop asked the parishes to develop forms for all children and teens participating in ministries and activities."

"What kind of forms?" Joe at least sounded curious rather than belligerent, and F.X. let out a deep breath.

"Oh, the usual." Riordan was leaning against the freezer chest when F.X. turned around. "Just standard permission slips, worded to take into account the way the legal system treats churches differently from public schools." He paused. "Contact forms, too, like the ones you have to fill out for the school in case your parents need to pick up the kids or help in the classroom while you're at work."

F.X. fought to hide a grin. Riordan was sneaky, all right.

"I've never filled out any forms like those." Joe shrugged. "Everybody in town knows Ma and Dad are my parents. They don't need a form to tell them that, not like the newcomers here."

"Years ago that was true." Riordan reached for the package of cold cuts. "Everybody's started worrying about getting sued these day, especially when dealing with children."

F.X. turned to the sink to wash his hands. "Is Parish Council worried about that, Riordan?"

"We have to be," he replied. "That's why Father wants to make sure that each family lists the people who might be picking up their children from events, whether it's a parent, sibling, other relative, or even a neighbor. Not to mention listing the people who can approve trips or other activities. If Mary said it was all right for Kara to stay late for a choir rehearsal and something happened, the church could be liable."

Joe snorted. "I'd never sue the parish. That's just not right."

"You wouldn't, but we can't require some parents to sign them and not all." Riordan looked through the bread laid out in front of the deli case. "Besides, like I said, you sign the school consent forms. This is the same thing."

"Forms, forms, and more forms." Joe made a face. "I get enough forms at work, and now I have to do more forms for the kids." He looked at the old clock on the wall. "Where is that boy?" He turned to the storeroom door. "Tim, get out here."

"Forms keep people like me in business, I'm afraid." Riordan chuckled as he put a loaf of rye bread on the counter next to the cold cuts. "But if it's really that much of a problem, I can draw up some paperwork that gives your parents the power to act in cases like that if you're not available. Once you put it on file with the schools and the parish, you wouldn't have to fill out a separate form each time."

When Joe didn't respond right away, F.X. jumped in. "I don't know about that..." He paused. "I know the forms are problematic, but I don't know if it's worth what it would cost to get-"

"Oh no, no cost." Riordan shook his head. "I've been working on this project long enough that I have some draft forms that are almost exactly what you need at the office. I couldn't charge you for something that's already done." He pulled out his wallet. "I'll bring it by your office, Joe, on my way back from court tomorrow. Your secretary can witness it, and then I'll bring it by here tomorrow. F.X., do you think if we made it lunchtime, Mary could be down here?" He grinned. "I can pick up a couple of your special sandwiches and surprise Becca with a late lunch after her class lets out."

F.X. shook his head as he rang up the purchases. "You two." He smiled. "Sure, Mary can be down here. Just don't tell her you're surprising Becca, or she'll start asking why you two don't get married already." He wasn't surprised at his friend's eye roll.

"Mary's a hopeless romantic." Riordan collected his change. "So, does that sound good?"

Joe nodded. "Yeah, sure. Whatever makes it easier." He growled. "That boy." He shook his head. "Dad, I'm going to just go get him, then go see if Ma and Kara are back. I'll make sure the latch catches on the back door." The younger man waved and headed into the storeroom.

F.X. waited a minute, then looked at Riordan. "You never fail to amaze me."

Riordan grinned. "It's all sleight of hand and psychology... and a really good knowledge of the law." He dropped his voice to just above a whisper. "I'll make sure the form is worded so you two can talk to teachers and sign off on activity forms. Maybe if you can talk to them about how things are going for Tim at school, alert them to your concerns at home, you can find a solution."

F.X. nodded. "Thanks. You're a good friend." He paused. "And probably a really bad enemy to have."

"You know me," Riordan said as he picked up the paper bag. "I do what I can to make things right — you're fine as long as you're on that side of the line." He winked and headed out.

As F.X. watched him go, he made a note to talk to Liz as soon as the paperwork was on file at the school. She could help him set up a discreet meeting with Tim's middle school teachers, too. This would only work if Joe didn't find out he was talking to the teachers, but it still was worth the risk. Whatever it took for both kids, he'd do it. If Joe found out, well, he'd deal with that when the time came.

THROWN OUT: STORIES FROM EXETER

INTRICATE DANCE

February 1969

Becca pulled her hat down over her ears, then shoved her gloved hands in the pockets of her jacket as she walked downtown. Days like this, she missed being near the coast. It didn't get quite as cold there. Not too cold to keep her from a night with her... well, whatever Riordan was. She refused to classify their relationship — wasn't even sure she wanted to call it a relationship. So far, he'd let her do that.

The stairs that led to Riordan's apartment over the law office were icy, even though she could hear the gritty salt crunching underfoot. She gripped the wooden railing all the way up. She shivered as she waited for him to answer her knock. Becca hunched down into her coat and knocked again. She could see a light in the window, so he had been home at some point after work. Becca was about to leave when she heard him call that he was coming.

"It's after six already?" Riordan opened the door for her. "I'm so sorry, Becca. I got caught up in a case and lost track of time." He took her coat and hung it on a peg by the door as she took off her boots. He still wore his tie, his shirt sleeves rolled up to his elbows. "Give me a minute to change, and we can go."

Becca put her hand on his arm. "We don't have to go anywhere." She wrapped her arms around herself. "It's freezing outside, and you've got a fireplace. We can just get pizza or Chinese and stay in."

He shook his head. "You wanted to go to that art exhibit in Worcester."

She shrugged. "We can always go this weekend. It will be there until next week."

He wrapped an arm around her shoulders and led her into the main room. "Let me change, and then I'll go get a pizza. There's beer in the refrigerator or wine on the counter." He rejoined her a few minutes later, now wearing a heavy wool sweater and jeans, and took a seat next to her on the couch.

"So, what's so interesting that you forgot about our date?" She tucked her legs up under her as she turned to face him.

Riordan hesitated. "It's a divorce case." He paused again. "I'm representing her. He's pretty powerful locally, and it's going to get ugly."

"How ugly?"

Riordan ran a hand through his hair. "My father wouldn't touch it. At least three other lawyers in town have told me I'm crazy for taking it on."

"But you're taking it anyway." Becca rested her elbows on her knees. "Tilting at windmills again?" She grinned.

"Just trying to make sure everybody plays by the same rules." He dropped his head back on the couch. "I've got an eyewitness who saw him beating her and enough medical evidence to show it wasn't the first time."

She straightened up. "And nobody else would take the case?"

Riordan shook his head. "Her husband's made it clear he's going to fight this. Getting a judge to agree to a divorce can be tricky anyway. Getting one to agree when the husband is fighting every step of the way? Almost impossible."

Becca stood up and started pacing. "That's ridiculous. Stupid, patriarchal, out-dated-" She growled. "What does he have to do, kill her first?"

"Becca."

"No, this is crazy." She crossed her arms and faced him. "This isn't some 1950s Leave It To Beaver world where everything's shiny and happy, and things like this just make it worse."

"Becca."

She fisted her hands on her hips. "You know if he wanted a divorce, she'd be stuck. He'd find a way to get it or just cheat his way around. Stupid men."

"Becca."

She stopped. "What?"

"You're right." Riordan pushed up to standing. "It's not right, and it's not fair. And if you keep trying to argue with nobody, the pizza place is going to close." He walked over and wrapped his arms around her. "This stupid man is going to pick up a pizza while you toast your frozen feet by the fire."

She leaned into him. "I'm not angry at you."

"I know." He smiled. "After three years, I know when you're mad at me and when you're just mad."

Becca rested her head on his shoulder. "I just... My mother always insisted I needed to find a man. Now that she's gone, my sister's doing the same thing. But they both were the same way — his word was law, no matter what. I'm not doing that. And I hate that everything is set up to make it easy for men to have everything and I have to fight three times as hard to get half as far."

She felt him rest his head on hers, his arms holding her close. "Nobody said life was fair." She felt his shoulders shrug, and her eyes stung.

"Nobody said I had to accept it, either."

"I hope you don't." Riordan stepped back, but kept his hands on her shoulders. "You argue more than almost any lawyer I've faced in court, and you win at least half the time.

You've never once accepted anything you didn't like. You shouldn't." He rubbed his hands over her arms. "Just do me one favor?"

She nodded.

"Remember my windmill-tilting before you lump me in with everybody else?"

Becca slid her hands around his neck and stepped close so she could whisper in his ear. "If you weren't tilting at windmills, we wouldn't be here now."

March 1969

Riordan walked into the antiquated building that housed the art department on campus, looking for one particular brunette. The open lobby and central hall were crowded with students and faculty for the opening reception, and even his height didn't make it easy to pick through the hordes for the one face he wanted to see. He'd changed into more casual clothes before leaving his apartment, but compared to the college crowd, he felt unbearably formal in slacks, a navy wool blazer, and a button-down shirt.

He started working his way through the space, pausing as people he knew from town stopped him to chat. More than one wondered what he was doing there, but he managed to brush off the questions.

When he finally saw her in the back corner, her paintings on the walls behind her, he smiled. He should have thought to find her work first, then look for her. He'd remember next time.

She had her back to him as she spoke with a few people Riordan didn't recognize. They must be from the college, because he knew they weren't from town. And Exeter State wasn't prestigious enough to attract people from outside the area for a student art show — even if his favorite artist was one of the featured exhibitors.

He walked up behind her and studied her paintings while he waited for her to finish. The colors were bold, demanding attention through their presence — just like the artist who painted them. Before he could examine the landscape in front of him more closely, he could hear the people behind him excusing themselves. He turned and stepped close behind her.

"So, I hear there's a beautiful, talented artist who has a show tonight..." He bent down close to her ear as he spoke and was rewarded when she jumped and spun around.

"I thought you said you had to work late." She pulled him into a hug.

Becca stepped back, looked at him, and rolled her eyes. "You played me. You didn't have to work late. You just wanted to sneak up on me." When he just smiled at her, she put her hands on her hips and glared at him for a second before laughing. "Sneak." She wrapped an arm around his waist. "So, what do you think?"

He pulled her close, arm across her shoulders. "I think you are much more interesting than writing law briefs." He pointed to a piece on the other wall, one with softer colors and edges than the landscape. "So, Madam Artist, tell me about that piece."

"Riordan." The familiar voice had his hand tensing briefly on Becca's shoulder.

"Hi, Dad." He turned to face his father. "Where's Ma?"

"She didn't feel up to coming." His father was still dressed in the three-piece suit he'd worn to the office, complete with a handkerchief in the breast pocket. Riordan suddenly felt entirely too casual. "And this is Rebecca, I presume?"

"Becca, meet my father." He looked to her, then across to his dad. "Dad, this is Becca Stone."

"It's nice to meet you, Mr. Boyle," she said, offering her hand. "I'm sorry to hear Mrs. Boyle is under the weather."

His father shook her hand but his expression, as he scanned her flowered bell-bottoms and bright green sweater, reminded Riordan of the the summer a skunk had gotten spooked by a dog and sprayed the side of their office building. "You're not quite what I expected." He paused. "Are you a graduate student here?"

Becca shook her head. "This is my senior year." She looked up at Riordan, and he realized his hand had tightened on her shoulder.

"Sorry," he muttered. Riordan turned to his father. "Are you enjoying the show?"

His father looked around. "This work is the closest I've seen to something that actually looks like art." He shook his head. "I believe your mother has some of your childhood drawings that are better than some of the things I see here."

"Now, Riordan." The voice came from behind his father. "Art comes in all different forms, or so they say."

"Fitzgerald." Riordan kept his voice emotionless. "I didn't expect to see you at a college art exhibit."

"The town is considering showcasing some of the pieces in Town Hall after this exhibit ends. I had to see if the work would be appropriate." The selectman's dark hair was slicked back, his suit as impeccable as Riordan's dad's.

Becca stepped forward. "It's nice to meet you, Mr. Fitzgerald, but you're mistaken. Mr. Boyle was the one questioning the artistic value of the pieces on display, not Riordan."

Riordan snorted. "Sorry, Becca. I should have been more specific." He motioned to his dad. "This is my father, Riordan Seamus Boyle, Jr."

Becca turned to him and lifted an eyebrow. "And you're Riordan the third? You never mentioned that."

"Riordan Seamus Boyle, III, Esquire? How pompous do you want me to get?" He turned back to his father and Fitzgerald. "If you're looking for something more representational, try the back wall in the rotunda — I saw some watercolors there that might suit Town Hall."

"No, I rather think I'd look right here." Fitzgerald smirked. "But don't let me disturb your discussion with this girl."

Riordan ignored the crawl up his spine at Fitzgerald's words as he turned to his father. "Dad?"

"I think I'll do that, son. It was nice to meet you, Rebecca." But he didn't shake her hand as he left, and Riordan knew he was going to hear about Becca in the morning. Too bad he didn't have any hearings scheduled that would keep him out of the office.

As his father walked off, Riordan felt Becca glare at him. She opened her mouth, and he shook his head, then tipped it toward Fitzgerald's back. Becca sighed, but went back to the previous topic. "Riordan Seamus? Can you get any more Irish than that?"

"My great-grandfather was born in Ireland and came over during the potato famine." He took her hand and steered her away from Fitzgerald. "Everybody in my grandparents' generation has Irish first names. Mine just got passed down."

She shook her head and lowered her voice. "So what's with the condescending idiot back there?"

He sighed. "Remember that case nobody would take?"

Her eyes widened. "That's him?" She wrinkled her nose. "I shouldn't have bothered to be polite."

Riordan choked back a snicker, then sobered. "Don't mess with him, Becca. Trust me on this one."

Before she could reply, he saw Fitzgerald approaching and shook his head slightly.

"My dear, I must compliment you on your work. It's stunning." Fitzgerald looked at her, then Riordan. "Now, Riordan, you've been keeping secrets. How did you meet this talented young girl?"

"Hardly a girl." Riordan forced himself to keep his voice light. "But I agree, Becca is a talented woman."

"Especially for somebody her age." Fitzgerald's grin held all the warmth of a shark. "I didn't realize you had such a... taste for girls, Riordan."

The crawling feeling on his spine turned into a tap-dance. But before he could reply, Becca spoke.

"What are you implying, Mr. Fitzgerald?" She stepped closer to the selectman until they were nose to nose, or nose to chest, since he had a good six inches on her. "I can promise you, I'm not only an adult, I'm above the legal drinking age."

"And how long have you known Riordan?" Fitzgerald looked down at her. "It would be a shame if the state bar association got a report about conduct unbecoming over inappropriate behavior with somebody underage."

Riordan could feel the back of his neck start to heat at Fitzgerald's words. "Fitzgerald-"

"Oh, Becca, there you are." An older man walked up. "Professor Grant is looking for you." He motioned for her to follow him, and she did, but not before throwing another glare at Fitzgerald.

As soon as she was out of earshot, Riordan stepped close to Fitzgerald so nobody could hear. "You're fishing for something you won't find, Fitzgerald. You have an issue with me representing your wife, you take it up with me. Don't go dragging anybody else into this." He walked off without waiting for a reply. He tried to distract himself with the rest of the exhibit, but finally gave up and left.

Instead of going home, he decided to go to Becca's apartment. He could use his key; she wouldn't mind. They needed to talk anyway, and if Fitzgerald followed her, saw him going in with her tonight, he'd try to use it. But the idea of the man following her home wouldn't leave his brain. He picked up the phone and dialed, muttering at how long it took the rotary dial to return to its original position. At least Exeter had finally done away with party lines a few years earlier. The whole neighborhood didn't need to hear this call.

It took just a minute to get Billy O'Meara on the phone at the station and just another minute to outline the situation.

"Do you think you can keep an eye on her as she walks home?" Riordan asked, leaning against the counter in the kitchenette. "Or mention it to the beat officer over there?"

"I can't do anything while she's on campus," the police officer said. "That's the campus force's territory. But I can wander over and keep an eye out. My buddies and I have been doing that for Eileen, too."

When Riordan got off the phone, he felt marginally better. Still, it wasn't until Becca walked in an hour later that he really relaxed. She hung her coat on the closet doorknob and pulled off her boots, balancing on one leg as she pulled the other boot off.

"So, did you have anything to do with the town cop I saw a few times on my way home?" She looked over at him.

Riordan sighed. "Are you mad?"

"Depends on why you did it." She straightened and crossed her arms.

"After you left, I told off Fitzgerald. He doesn't take that well, and he's fighting this case hard. Now that he knows getting to you would get to me, I didn't want to give him a chance."

Becca didn't say anything, just looked at him.

"Billy — the officer — his sister's the eyewitness against Fitzgerald. I knew he'd keep an eye on you, just the way he has Eileen." Riordan ran a hand through his hair. "Fitzgerald's a big man. If he attacked you, he could do some serious damage. I didn't want to risk that, risk you."

Becca unfolded her arms and walked over to sit on the ragged couch next to him, folding her legs beneath her. "I'm not a china doll."

"You didn't sign on for my enemies, either." He hesitated. "He's already threatening to use our relationship to try and stop the case."

"Let him threaten." Becca shrugged. "He's not going to scare me. And if you dare drop this case because you're afraid I might get hurt..." She took a deep breath. "I can fight my own fights. You just make sure he doesn't win this."

JENNIE COUGHLIN

April 1969

Becca stuffed her sketchpad into her book bag and headed downtown. This was her one free day at the college, and she usually spent it in her studio. This was just a different approach, a chance for her to do some live sketching. Still she knew she was just making excuses. After all the problems Riordan had faced preparing for this case, she wanted to be there for him. She wanted to see Fitzgerald get what he deserved. She pedaled her battered bike as fast as she could, then rolled it into the alley next to the courthouse. Last summer she had used it as her canvas for the assignment to paint something in the style of Van Gogh's Starry Night. The additional benefit being she never worried about it getting stolen. Everybody knew it was hers.

She made her way into the courtroom, its wood-paneled walls lined with people. She found an unoccupied corner and pulled out her sketchpad. She listened to the arguments on both sides as she started drawing, shading and cross-hatching to get the right effects. Riordan was dressed in a full three-piece suit, his rust-colored hair slicked back to tame it. Mrs. Fitzgerald sat at Riordan's table, her straw-colored hair coiled neatly at the base of her neck. The freckles on her pale skin stood out; her pale blue dress reminded Becca of the Mary statue outside St. Brigid's.

On the other side of the courtroom, Mr. Fitzgerald appeared to be bored. His navy suit and crimson tie were crisp and fresh as he leaned back in the chair. But the skin around his mouth was tight, and his fingers drummed on his knee. When Riordan called a teenager to the stand, Becca noticed Fitzgerald clenched his hand briefly into a fist, then relaxed it as the bailiff administered the oath.

"Can you state your name for the court?" Riordan's voice was calm, almost gentle.

"Eileen O'Meara, sir." The teen's dark hair curled about her shoulders, contrasting with her pale skin. Becca jotted notes on the side of the sketch, wanting to capture the contrasts in color, the bright blue of her eyes and deep forest green of her dress.

"You clean the Fitzgeralds' house, is that correct?"

"Yes, sir." She nodded. "I have for three years, since I turned 15. I'm saving my money to attend nursing school in the fall."

"How often are you there?"

"Mr. Fitzgerald pays me to come by three days a week to do the heavy cleaning," she replied. She sat tall in the witness box, but never looked at the man.

"What time do you normally stop by?" As Riordan led Eileen through her testimony, Mr. Fitzgerald's lawyer objected.

"Your honor, Mr. Boyle has not demonstrated how this is relevant." The lawyer was just a few inches shorter than Riordan, still close to six feet. Becca had seen him around town, but had never met him.

"Your honor, if you will allow a few more questions, Miss O'Meara's testimony will clearly be relevant." Riordan's at-ease appearance contrasted with the coiled energy of Fitzgerald's lawyer.

"Very well, but make it a very few number of questions." The judge sat back in his chair.

"Miss O'Meara, what time did you stop by on February 24?"

"I had some meetings with teachers after school, and I didn't get to the Fitzgeralds' house until after four o'clock." She took a deep breath. "Mr. Fitzgerald arrived home an hour and a half later."

"And what did you hear?"

As Riordan tried to draw out Eileen's testimony despite constant objections from Fitzgerald's lawyer, Becca focused on Mrs. Fitzgerald. At each objection, she shrank down a little more. Fitzgerald sat up a bit straighter, and Becca could see the corners of his lips twitching. She looked down to realize she'd pressed the pencil so hard into the paper, she'd snapped off the tip. She took a deep breath and put the pencil down. Riordan could do this. He could get the judge to agree that Mrs. Fitzgerald deserved a divorce from her abusive husband no matter how much clout the selectman had. Riordan would succeed. He had to.

~~~~~~~~~~~

Riordan could hear the whispers in the courtroom, if not the actual words, but he blocked it out. All that mattered was getting the facts on the table, making the case clear enough that Judge Bachmann would have no choice but to grant Anne Fitzgerald's petition. He stood between Eileen O'Meara and Fitzgerald.

"And what did you hear?"

The girl took a deep breath. "At first, I didn't know what it was. I had just finished hanging the laundry to dry in the basement, and the clothes blocked the sounds. I finished and went upstairs to wash the floors."

"Objection, Your Honor. The witness has not answered the question." Opposing counsel Joe Kerrigan was quick to speak when Eileen paused.

"Your Honor, Miss O'Meara was just getting to that." Riordan made sure to sound cooperative and calm.

"Miss O'Meara?" Judge Bachmann turned to the girl.

"Yes, sir." Eileen nodded. "I was on the third step when I heard a crack and something hit the floor. I crept up the steps, afraid it might have been a burglar or some other bad man."

"And what did you see when you looked into the kitchen?" Riordan watched for signs the girl would buckle under the pressure and worried about the white marks around her knuckles as she squeezed her folded hands together.

"I saw-" She took a deep breath. "I saw Mrs. Fitzgerald on the floor, her hand to her cheek. Mr. Fitzgerald was standing over her."

Riordan knew the first question Kerrigan would ask on cross-examination and moved to cut off that line of questioning. "What else did you see?"

"Mrs. Fitzgerald had a red mark on her cheek, shaped like a hand."

"What else did you see?"

"Mr. Fitzgerald grabbed her hair and pulled her up." Eileen looked over at Anne Fitzgerald. "Mrs. Fitzgerald screamed, and he slapped her across the face."

Riordan continued to coax the details out of Eileen, even though he could sense the shame Anne was radiating. He wished they could have closed the courtroom for this hearing, but when he had petitioned for that concession Bachmann refused to heed it.

As he finished and returned to his seat during the cross-examination, he saw how small Anne was in her chair, her shoulders hunched and head bowed. When he sat, he leaned over and put his hand over hers. "I know this is painful, but we need to make sure he can't get out of this," he whispered in her ear.

Anne just nodded and kept her gaze on her lap.

Riordan worked his way methodically through the rest of the case, including his cross-examination of Fitzgerald. The man disgusted him, using his money and power to shield himself from the consequences of his actions. Not this time, though. Not if Riordan had anything to say about it.

As Riordan made his closing argument to the judge, he watched Bachmann's face for clues. Nothing. The man was good at concealing his feelings.

When Fitzgerald's lawyer had rested his case, Riordan waited for the judge to call the recess while he deliberated. d

"Please stand," Bachmann said instead. "I will deliver my verdict."

Riordan swallowed, but stood motioning Anne to stand as well.

"I have considered all the facts presented to me today and have come to a ruling." Bachman looked at both

Fitzgeralds and both lawyers, his gaze focusing on each in turn. "Mrs. Fitzgerald, despite the case your attorney has made, you continued to live in the same house as your husband while this alleged 'cruel and unusual punishment' was taking place, thus condoning his behavior. Under the laws of the state of Massachusetts, I cannot find him at fault. Your request for a divorce is not granted."

Riordan clenched his fists as the judge read out the verdict. He'd hoped the quick court date would avoid this outcome.

As Bachmann gaveled for recess, Fitzgerald walked over. "Come, Anne." He held out his hand. "Now that this silliness is over, it's time to go home."

She shook her head.

Fitzgerald stepped closer. "Anne, you're coming with me."

"No." Her voice was barely audible. "I'm not."

"You have nowhere to go. No family in the area. You have no choice." Fitzgerald pitched his voice low, and Riordan could see the people in the front row straining to hear.

"The lady said she's not going with you." Riordan stepped between them. "You won, Fitzgerald. Now leave her alone."

Instead, the selectman tried to push Riordan aside, shoving him in the chest. "She's my wife."

"But she's not your punching bag." He grabbed at Fitzgerald's wrists, but the man evaded and grabbed at Riordan's lapels.

"Hey, break it up." The bailiff stepped between them. Riordan walked Anne over to a woman from the next parish. Father Gallagher had talked to the priest there and arranged for Anne to stay with her after the trial, until she could find her own place. After a few words, he walked them out to a side door where the woman had parked. When he returned to the main lobby, Fitzgerald was gone.

Becca was waiting outside the courthouse when Riordan finally walked out, his coat collar still crumpled and tie askew.

"Becca?"

She just held out the sketchbook, open to one she'd done as Fitzgerald was attacking him.

Riordan flushed and ducked his head. "I couldn't let him hurt her any more."

"Who knew Exeter had an Atticus Finch of its very own?"

Riordan shook his head. "I'm no hero, Becca."

"To Mrs. Fitzgerald, you are." She tugged him along toward the diner.

Riordan shook his head. "She needed help, and I thought I could help her. Nobody else was willing to take her case."

"Nobody else was willing to make her husband into an enemy." Becca stopped and turned to face him. "You remember when we met?"

He nodded. "Bobby Kennedy had been shot, and you were watching the news from the sidewalk outside Hogan's store."

"And later that week, Teddy described his brother at the funeral. He called him, 'a good and decent man, who saw wrong and tried to right it, saw suffering and tried to heal it, saw war and tried to stop it.' Now as far as I know, you haven't tried to stop a war, but the rest of that description? As far as I'm concerned, it matches you pretty darn well." She looked at him, but he looked away.

"Becca, don't. I'm not like Atticus or Bobby Kennedy. I'm just a small town lawyer." He pulled his hand back and started walking. "There have been times I could have done something and didn't." She had to hurry to keep up with him. "Times I should have done something and didn't. I can't go back. All I can do is try to make up for my cowardice."

JENNIE COUGHLIN

June 1969

Riordan headed over to campus, hoping to catch Becca at her studio. She usually spent most Saturday mornings there painting, and he was hoping to convince her to join him for a picnic lunch once she was done.

He'd thought of asking her about the idea Thursday, but she hated planning ahead. She always claimed it was more fun to just see what life had in store. There were times when his schedule was busy that she would consent to making plans, but he'd grown to like surprising her more than he'd ever expected. When he walked in, she had her back to the door. The room was crammed with canvases and paints, more than he would have thought could fit in a space so small he could stand in the middle and touch each wall. As she wielded a brush, he leaned against the doorframe, content just to watch. As many times as he'd seen her sketch while they were out, as many paintings as he'd viewed, he never got over being impressed with her skill. She used paint the way he used words, always knowing when to add more and when to tread sparingly.

When she straightened up, put the brush down, and twisted side to side, he called to her.

"Hey," she said. "What's the occasion?" She wiped her hands on the front of her tattered jeans, the orange layering over a dozen colors already there.

He held up the basket in his hand. "Picnic? I thought we could relax on the Quad for a while."

She grinned. "Picnic, yes, but not on the Quad — we'll get trampled by the Frisbee games. I have a better place." She picked up a bottle of turpentine and waved for him to step aside, then headed down the hall to the restroom. When she returned, Becca led the way out the back door of the building and down behind the campus chapel. The quiet courtyard was shaded, surrounded by faded brick walls designed to allow light to dance across the space. Becca led him to a grassy corner, and he spread out the blanket he'd brought along.

As they stretched out, passing food back and forth, he studied his friend's face. She wasn't classically beautiful. Her jaw was too square, her hair untidy. A streak of yellow paint had dried on her cheek. But her energy never failed to make him smile, even when she was arguing like opposing counsel.

Becca was quiet now, though.

"Penny for your thoughts."

She sighed. "I heard about Mrs. Fitzgerald."

He nodded. "He's in jail for assault now." Riordan rolled over on his back. "The appeals court reversed the original ruling yesterday and granted the divorce. That's what set him off."

Becca reached over and turned his head to face her. "It's not your fault. You were the first one to try and help her."

"It wasn't enough." He pulled away. "The doctors said she'll probably always walk with a limp. He broke her leg in three places." He tipped his head and cracked his neck. "I can't understand how he could treat her that way."

Becca nudged him to sit up, then moved behind him. Her strong hands started to knead his shoulders. "It wasn't an equal partnership. I don't know that it ever can be."

"There was nothing equal about the Fitzgeralds' marriage. That doesn't mean it's impossible." Riordan paused. "My father loves my mother and would never raise his hand to her."

He could feel her hair brush the back of his neck and assumed she was shaking her head. "No, I'm sure he wouldn't. But an equal partnership isn't defined by a lack of abuse. Women don't have the same protection and rights under the law. That's the part I can't live with."

He stifled a sigh of disappointment and forced himself to keep his tone light. "So no point in looking at the rings in Pat Dolan's window?"

Her hands stilled. "Riordan..." Becca slid her arms around his shoulders. "I love you. You're the best man I know. I just... It's not you, it's marriage."

He took a deep breath, knowing he needed to ask, even if he didn't like her answer. "Can you tell me... I want you in my life, and I can't imagine a future without you there. I don't need the ring or the vows or the piece of paper. But..." He hesitated. "I do need to know if you feel the same way." He waited for her answer, hoping it would be the one he wanted.

"I do." She kissed the side of his neck. "Just don't expect me to say those two words in front of a priest."

He turned around to take her in his arms, his best friend and lover. He would take her however he could get her for as long as she would have him.

ABOUT THE AUTHOR

Jennie Coughlin was raised in Franklin, Massachusetts. Her first short story was the final project for a local history unit in middle school, and it sparked a love of both fiction writing and local history that continues to this day. She graduated from the University of Missouri with a bachelor's degree in journalism. She has worked as a reporter and editor for community newspapers based in Massachusetts and Virginia.

Coughlin has lived in small towns her entire life and draws heavily on that inspiration for the Exeter series. A life of living in small college towns with lots of history and strong arts communities comes through in her stories about Exeter, a small mill town in the Blackstone Valley of Massachusetts. The name is a nod to her hometown's history, but Exeter isn't based on Franklin or any of the other small towns she's lived in — reality in those places is far too unbelievable to make good fiction.

She posts snippets of Exeter stories weekly on her site (http://jenniecoughlin.wordpress.com) as part of the ongoing Rory's Story Cubes Challenge, chats on Twitter — @jenniecoughlin — and appreciates your comments, which can be e-mailed to jenniecoughlin28@gmail.com.

Made in the USA
Lexington, KY
05 October 2011